THE PAWN

SKYE WARREN

Every pawn is a potential queen.

– James Mason

PROLOGUE

T HE PARTY SPILLS over with guests, from the ballroom to the front lawn. It's nighttime, but the house is lit up, bright as the sun. All around me diamonds glitter. We've reached that tipping point where everyone is sloshed enough to smile, but not so much they start to slur. There's almost too many people, almost too much alcohol. Almost too much wealth in one room.

It reminds me of Icarus, with his wings of feather and wax. If Icarus had a five-hundred-person guest list for his graduation party. It reminds me of flying too close to the sun.

I snag a flute of champagne from one of the servers, who pretends not to see. The bubbles tickle my nose as I take a detour through the kitchen. Rosita stands at the stove, stirring her world-famous jambalaya in a large cast iron pot. The spices pull me close.

I reach for a spoon. "Is it ready yet?"

She slaps my hand away. "You'll ruin your

pretty dress. It'll be ready when it's ready."

We have caterers who make food for all our events, but since this is my graduation party, Rosita agreed to make my favorite dish. She's going to spoon some onto little puff pastry cups and call it a canape.

I try to pout, but everything is too perfect for that. Only one thing is missing from this picture. I give her a kiss on the cheek. "Thanks, Rosita. Have you seen Daddy?"

"Where he always is, most likely."

That's what I'm afraid of. Then I'm through the swinging door that leads into the private side of the house. I pass Gerty, our event planner, who's muttering about guests who aren't on the invite list.

I head up the familiar oak staircase, breathing in the scent of our house. There's something so comforting about it. I'm going to miss everything when I leave for college.

At the top of the stairs, I hear men's voices.

That isn't unusual. I'm around the corner from Daddy's office. There are always men coming to meet with him. Half the people he works with are downstairs right now. But he promised no work tonight, and I'm going to hold him to it, even if I have to drag him downstairs myself.

"How dare you accuse me of…"

The venom in the words stops me on the landing. That doesn't sound like a regular business meeting. Things might get tense around a contract, but there's plenty of back slapping and football talk before and after.

More heated words hover just below the noise of the party, ominous and indistinguishable. I twist my hands together, about to turn around. I won't bother him after all.

A man rounds the corner, almost colliding into me.

I gasp, taking a step back. There's nothing behind me. *The stairs!* Then two hands grasp my arms, hauling me back onto steady ground. I have only a glimpse of furious golden eyes, almost feline, definitely feral. Then he's sweeping past me down the stairs. I cling to the carved banister, my knees weak.

It's another minute before I can detach myself from the wood railing. My breath still feels shuddery from that near miss, from that man's hands on my bare arms. I find Daddy pacing inside his office. He glances up at me with a strange expression—almost like panic.

"Daddy?"

"There you are, Avery. I'm sorry. I know I said no work—"

"Who was that?"

A cloud crosses over his expression. Only now, in the lamp's eerie glow, do I notice the lines on his face. Deeper than ever. "Don't worry about him. This night is all about you."

Now that I've started noticing his appearance, I can't stop. His hair. All salt now. No more pepper. "You know I don't need all this. This party. Everything. You don't have to work so hard."

The smile that crosses his face is wistful. "What would I do if I wasn't working?"

I shrug, because it doesn't matter. My friend Krista's dad plays golf every single day. Harper's mom is on her fourth husband. Anything but plant himself behind a desk, eyes soft with strain. "You could date or something."

He laughs, looking more like himself. "You're the only girl in my life, sweetie. Now, come on. Let's join the party before they trash the place."

His arm around my shoulders pulls me close, and I curl into his jacket. I breathe in the comforting smell of him—the faint scent of cigar smoke, even though he swears he's quit. I lay my head on his shoulder as we pass the chessboard where we play together.

"I'll miss our games."

He kisses my temple. "Not as much as I'll miss you."

"You could download an app on your phone. We could play online."

"I'm lucky if I can make calls on this damn thing," he says, laughing. His expression darkens when he looks at the screen of his phone, reading the text across a white popup background. "Sweetheart, I have to call someone."

Disappointment burns down my throat. Of course he's a busy man. Most of my friends barely know their dads. I'm lucky he's always made time for me. No matter how crazy things get at his business, he always makes time for our chess games. Every week.

I kiss his cheek, seeing the age spots on leathery skin for the first time.

Downstairs I find Justin by following the sound of his laugh. It's a big, booming laugh that I suspect he's practiced. However it happened, it's infectious. I'm already grinning when I enter the room.

He holds out his hand to me. "The woman of the hour."

I fold into his side, tickled by the champagne

in my bloodstream and the relief of being down-stairs. Whatever happened in that office was tense. Dark. "I was just checking on Daddy."

"Working," Justin guesses.

"Unfortunately."

"Well, I guess you're stuck with me," Justin says, winking at the couple he was talking to. I recognize them as a famous neurosurgeon and his wife, parents to a man running for the state senate seat.

I make my introductions to them. Of course this party isn't only for my high school gradua-tion. Like all the other parties in Tanglewood society, it's about networking. For my father. For Justin, who has big plans to follow his father's footsteps into politics.

"Salutatorian," Justin's saying. "You should have heard her speech about the way the things we do now are the myths of the future."

The man smiles, somewhat indulgent. "She'll be a great asset to you, son."

I manage to keep a pleasant expression, even though I hope to be more than an asset. I want to be his partner. He knows that, doesn't he? Justin has that public smile, the one that's too bright and too white. The one that doesn't mean anything.

By the time we make our excuses, my cheeks

hurt from smiling.

Justin pulls me behind a screen, nuzzling my neck. "Maybe we can sneak up to your room."

"Oh," I say, a catch in my breath. "I think Daddy will be down soon..."

"He won't find out," he murmurs, his hands sliding over my dress, under it. We're not visible to the party, but anyone could walk back here. My heart pounds. His hands are soft and grasping—and for some reason my mind flashes to the man at the top of the stairs, his firm grip on my arms.

"Justin, I—"

"Come on. You turned eighteen two weeks ago."

And okay, I did use that as an excuse before. Because I didn't feel ready. And it has nothing to do with how old I am or how much I love Justin. Maybe if my mother were still alive, if she could have told me the secrets of being a woman. The internet is a terrifying teacher.

I turn in his arms, pushing him to arms' length. "I love you."

He frowns. "Avery."

"But it wasn't just being seventeen. It's everything. I want... I want to wait."

His eyes narrow, and I'm sure he's going to

say no. He's going to storm off. *What if I ruined everything?*

By degrees he seems to relax. "Okay."

"Okay?"

He sighs. "I'm not happy about it, but I'm willing to wait. You're worth waiting for."

My throat feels tight. I know it's a lot to ask for, but he's the best boyfriend I can imagine. And Daddy loves him, which is a huge plus. This fall I'll start school at Smith College, the same private all-girls college where Harper's going. Everything is perfect.

That's how it feels in this moment, like flying.

I have no idea that in less than a year I'll fall from the sky.

CHAPTER ONE

WIND WHIPS AROUND my ankles, flapping the bottom of my black trench coat. Beads of moisture form on my eyelashes. In the short walk from the cab to the stoop, my skin has slicked with humidity left by the rain.

Carved vines and ivy leaves decorate the ornate wooden door.

I have some knowledge of antique pieces, but I can't imagine the price tag on this one—especially exposed to the elements and the whims of vandals. I suppose even criminals know enough to leave the Den alone.

Officially the Den is a gentlemen's club, the old-world kind with cigars and private invitations. Unofficially it's a collection of the most powerful men in Tanglewood. Dangerous men. Criminals, even if they wear a suit while breaking the law.

A heavy brass knocker in the shape of a fierce lion warns away any visitors. I'm desperate enough to ignore that warning. My heart thuds in my chest and expands out, pulsing in my fingers, my toes. Blood rushes through my ears, drowning out the whoosh of traffic behind me.

I grasp the thick ring and knock—once, twice.

Part of me fears what will happen to me behind that door. A bigger part of me is afraid the door won't open at all. I can't see any cameras set into the concrete enclave, but they have to be watching. Will they recognize me? I'm not sure it would help if they did. Probably best that they see only a desperate girl, because that's all I am now.

The softest scrape comes from the door. Then it opens.

I'm struck by his eyes, a deep amber color—like expensive brandy and almost translucent. My breath catches in my throat, lips frozen against words like *please* and *help*. Instinctively I know they won't work; this isn't a man given to mercy. The tailored cut of his shirt, its sleeves carelessly rolled up, tells me he'll extract a price. One I can't afford to pay.

There should have been a servant, I thought. A butler. Isn't that what fancy gentlemen's clubs have? Or maybe some kind of a security guard. Even our house had a housekeeper answer the door—at least, before. Before we fell from grace.

Before my world fell apart.

The man makes no move to speak, to invite me in or turn me away. Instead he stares at me with vague curiosity, with a trace of pity, the way one might watch an animal in the zoo. That might be how the whole world looks to these men, who have more money than God, more power than the president.

That might be how I looked at the world, before.

My throat feels tight, as if my body fights this move, even while my mind knows it's the only option. "I need to speak with Damon Scott."

Scott is the most notorious loan shark in the city. He deals with large sums of money, and nothing less will get me through this. We have been introduced, and he left polite society by the time I was old enough to attend events regularly. There were whispers, even then, about the young man with ambition. Back then he had ties to the underworld—and now he's its king.

One thick eyebrow rises. "What do you want with him?"

A sense of familiarity fills the space between us even though I know we haven't met. This man is a stranger, but he looks at me as if he wants to know me. He looks at me as if he already does. There's an intensity to his eyes when they sweep over my face, as firm and as telling as a touch.

"I need…" My heart thuds as I think about all the things I need—a rewind button. One person in the city who doesn't hate me by name alone. "I need a loan."

He gives me a slow perusal, from the nervous slide of my tongue along my lips to the high neckline of my clothes. I tried to dress professionally—a black cowl-necked sweater and pencil skirt. His strange amber gaze unbuttons my coat, pulls away the expensive cotton, tears off the fabric of my bra and panties. He sees right through me, and I shiver as a ripple of awareness runs over my skin.

I've met a million men in my life. Shaken hands. Smiled. I've never felt as seen through as I do right now. Never felt like someone has turned me inside out, every dark secret exposed to the harsh light. He sees my weaknesses, and from the cruel set of his mouth, he likes them.

His lids lower. "And what do you have for collateral?"

Nothing except my word. That wouldn't be worth anything if he knew my name. I swallow past the lump in my throat. "I don't know."

Nothing.

He takes a step forward, and suddenly I'm

crowded against the brick wall beside the door, his large body blocking out the warm light from inside. He feels like a furnace in front of me, the heat of him in sharp contrast to the cold brick at my back. "What's your name, girl?"

The word *girl* is a slap in the face. I force myself not to flinch, but it's hard. Everything about him overwhelms me—his size, his low voice. "I'll tell Mr. Scott my name."

In the shadowed space between us, his smile spreads, white and taunting. The pleasure that lights his strange yellow eyes is almost sensual, as if I caressed him. "You'll have to get past me."

My heart thuds. He likes that I'm challenging him, and God, that's even worse. What if I've already failed? I'm free-falling, tumbling, turning over without a single hope to anchor me. Where will I go if he turns me away? What will happen to my father?

"Let me go," I whisper, but my hope fades fast.

His eyes flash with warning. "Little Avery James, all grown up."

A small gasp resounds in the space between us. He already knows my name. That means he knows who my father is. He knows what he's done. Denials rush to my throat, pleas for understanding. The hard set of his eyes, the broad strength of his shoulders tells me I won't find any mercy here.

I square my shoulders. I'm desperate but not broken. "If you know my name, you know I have friends in high places. Connections. A history in this city. That has to be worth something. That's my collateral."

Those connections might not even take my call, but I have to try something. I don't know if it will be enough for a loan or even to get me through the door. Even so, a faint feeling of family pride rushes over my skin. Even if he turns me away, I'll hold my head high.

Golden eyes study me. Something about the way he said *little Avery James* felt familiar, but I've never seen this man. At least I don't think we've met. Something about the otherworldly glow of those eyes whispers to me, like a melody I've heard before.

On his driver's license it probably says something mundane, like brown. But that word can never encompass the way his eyes seem almost luminous, orbs of amber that hold the secrets of the universe. *Brown* can never describe the deep golden hue of them, the indelible opulence in his fierce gaze.

"Follow me," he says.

Relief courses through me, flooding numb limbs, waking me up enough that I wonder what I'm doing here. These aren't men, they're animals. They're predators, and I'm prey. Why would I willingly walk inside?

What other choice do I have?

I step over the veined marble threshold.

The man closes the door behind me, shutting out the rain and the traffic, the entire city disappeared in one soft turn of the lock. Without another word he walks down the hall, deeper into the shadows. I hurry to follow him, my chin held high, shoulders back, for all the world as if I were an invited guest. Is this how the gazelle feels when she runs over the plains, a study in grace, poised for her slaughter?

The entire world goes black behind the staircase, only breath, only bodies in the dark. Then he opens another thick wooden door, revealing a dimly lit room of cherrywood and cut crystal, of leather and smoke. Barely I see dark eyes, dark suits. Dark men.

I have the sudden urge to hide behind the man with the golden eyes. He's wide and tall, with hands that could wrap around my waist. He's a giant of a man, rough-hewn and hard as stone.

Except he's not here to protect me. He could be the most dangerous of all.

A man blows out a breath, smoke curling from his lips. He wears a slate-gray vest and lavender tie. On another man it would have made him soft, but with the two-days' growth on a strong jaw, with the devilish glint in his black eyes he's pure masculine power.

Damon Scott.

"Who do we have here?" he says.

There are other men in the room, other suits, but I don't focus on them.

The man takes a seat near Damon, to the right of him and a little deeper in the shadows, his eyes turned to bronze in the dark. Like he's watching all of us, like he's set apart. I don't focus on him either.

"I'm Avery James," I say, lifting my chin. "And I'm here for a loan."

Damon drops his cigar into a ceramic dish on the side table. He leans forward, pressing his fingers together. "Avery James, as I live and breathe. I never expected you to visit me."

"Desperate times," I say because my predicament isn't a secret.

"Desperate measures," he says slowly, as if

tasting the words, treasuring them. "I'm not in the habit of giving money away for nothing, even to beautiful women."

I find myself searching the darkness for golden eyes. For courage? Whatever the reason, strength infuses me like a thick gulp of brandy. "What do you give money away for?"

Damon laughs suddenly, the rich sound filling the room. The other men chuckle along with him. I'm their source of entertainment. My cheeks flame.

The man with golden eyes doesn't crack a smile.

Damon leans forward, obsidian eyes glinting. "In return for even more money, beautiful. Which is why you have a problem. That high school diploma isn't going to count for much, not even from the best private school in the state."

It wouldn't. And who would hire a James when my father has just been convicted of fraud? Part of me still refuses to see the truth. I keep flinching away from it. Every time it hurts. "I'm smart. I'm willing to work. I'll figure out something. I just need time."

Time to keep the creditors at bay, time to pay for my father's medical care. Time to pray, because I don't have any other options.

"Time." He gives me a crooked grin. "And how much is that worth to you?"

My father's life. That's what hangs in the balance. "Everything."

Golden eyes watch me steadily, measuring me. Testing me.

Mr. Scott huffs an amused breath. "Why would I hand you twenty grand that I'm never going to see again, much less interest?"

More than twenty grand. I need fifty. *I need a miracle.* "Please. If you can't help me—"

"I can't," he says flatly.

Golden Eyes reclines, face half in shadow. "That's not quite true."

The whole room stills. Even Damon Scott pauses, as if seriously considering the words. Damon Scott is the richest man in the city, the most powerful. The most dangerous. Who can tell him what to do?

"Who are you?" I say, my voice shaking only a little.

"Does it matter?" Golden Eyes asks, his tone mocking.

Righteous anger mixes with desperation. I'm already in a free fall—why shouldn't I spread my arms? "Who are you?" I say again. "If you're going to decide my fate, I should at least know your name."

He leans forward, the light adding amber to his lambent gaze. "Gabriel," he says simply.

My heart stops.

Scott smiles, his eyes crinkling with pleasure. He's relishing this, anticipating it. It's almost sexual, the way he watches me. "Gabriel Miller. The man your father stole from."

Gabriel Miller smiles faintly. "The *last* man he stole from."

Oh, and he made sure my father could never steal again.

Never do *anything* again.

Pinpricks against my eyes. No, I can't cry in front of them. I can't fall apart at all, because my father is lying in a bed, unable to get up, hardly able to move—because of what this man did.

This is the man who turned my father in to the authorities.

This is the man who caused my family's fall from grace.

I push down the knot in my throat. "You—" A deep breath, because it's taking all my self-control not to launch myself at him. "You're a murderer."

If Scott is the king of the underworld, Gabriel Miller is a god. His empire extends across the southern states and even overseas. He buys and sells anything worth money—drugs, guns. People. My father warned me to stay away from him, but then why did he secretly take bribes? Why did he betray Gabriel Miller, knowing how dangerous he was?

My father isn't dead, but without a heavy dose of pain medicine, he wishes he were.

"I've killed men," Gabriel says, standing to full height. I can't help but step back a little. Would he hit me? Worse? His eyes narrow. "When they lie to me. When they steal from me."

Like my father did.

That same sense of falling turns my stomach. I know I should be terrified, and I am—but I've been locked up in a cage my whole life. Part of me enjoys the wind against my face. "I didn't steal from you."

Scott gives a short nod, acknowledging that horrible truth. "His money still paid for your pretty shoes, didn't it? The yoga classes that built that beautiful body?"

And my father paid a terrible price for that money. I still remember him bloodied, broken. Someone sent men to break him. Was it the men that my father double-crossed Gabriel Miller for?

Or was it Gabriel Miller who ordered my father beaten?

I force my shoulders back. "You said you could help me."

Whatever happens next, I'll face it with honor, with courage. With the same sense of strength I believe my father had. How had he taught me about honesty while lying the whole time? The James name used to mean something, and I'm trying to maintain the last shreds of our dignity.

"Take off the coat," Gabriel says, his tone almost mild.

Everything inside me turns cold, bones frozen, breath a cold blast of air in my lungs. "Why?"

"I want to see what I'm working with. Don't worry, girl. I'm not going to touch you."

With shaking hands I untie my coat and let it slide from my shoulders. There are indistinct murmurs from the men around me—approval, interest. I have the sudden sense that I'm in the center of a bullfight, a stadium full of spectators hungry for blood.

Finally I meet Gabriel's eyes, and what I see is a fire of desire, red and orange and yellow. The blaze scalds me from four feet away. The businesslike clothes I chose to wear don't show much of my skin, but they show all of my shape. The flame of his hunger licks over my breasts, my waist, down my legs.

"Lovely," Damon Scott murmurs. "But a beautiful body isn't enough. You need to know how to use it."

I shiver. He owns a string of strip clubs all over the city. "I can...learn."

Something flashes in Gabriel's eyes. "You don't know how to please a man, girl?"

There had been stolen kisses, furtive touches in the darkened hallways outside society parties. Justin had pushed me, but I had pushed back. Something had always kept me from letting him have sex with me. And then my family name was disgraced.

You have to understand, Avery. I want to be a senator someday. I can't do that married to a James now.

That was the day after the indictment.

In light of that impersonal phone call, I knew our relationship wasn't about respect. It wasn't about love either. Definitely not pleasure. No, I have no idea how to please a man.

"I'm a virgin," I say softly, sadly, because even if this ruins everything, I can't lie about it. Not when Gabriel Miller has confessed to killing men who lied.

Not when it would be so easy to confirm.

Damon Scott's eyes widen, and something sparks in them, interest where there had been only denial. "A virgin, Avery James? Are you serious?"

A flush turns my cheeks hot. It might seem strange for a nineteen-year-old woman not to have sex, but I went to St. Mary's Preparatory Academy in high school, an all-girl's Catholic school. My father was protective, only allowing me out at night to society events he also attended. By the time I left for college, I was already engaged to Justin.

Gabriel makes a low sound, almost a growl. "She's serious."

Damon Scott looks conflicted. "She's too young."

"You have younger girls dancing at your fucking clubs."

Except they aren't talking about dancing. The thought makes my heart stop. They're talking about selling my body for sex. My virginity. "No," I whisper. "I won't do it."

"You see," Damon Scott says. "She won't do it."

Gabriel's gaze sweeps over my body. He meets my eyes, his expression intent. "She doesn't have a choice. It's the most valuable thing she owns."

It's not a *thing*, I want to scream. This is my

body.

Except he's right. It's the most valuable thing I own—the only thing of any value left after the criminal fines and restitution had been paid, after the lawyers and the bill collectors.

Challenge burns in Gabriel's eyes. He knows how desperate I am. He's the one who made me this way. Does he enjoy seeing me brought low? I wasn't the one who betrayed him, but like Scott said, it was still his money paying for my tuition, my clothes.

"How much?" I ask, the hard knot in my stomach a sign I've already lost.

Damon Scott gives a small smile. "We'll have an auction."

I've been to auctions before—of paintings, antique furniture. The audience with their glasses of wine and numbered signs for bidding. I imagine myself up on the stage. "Who would attend?"

There's a hungry gleam in Damon Scott's eyes. "I know a good many men who'd love to teach you the art of pleasure."

I seriously doubt that I'll feel any pleasure with a strange man, one who prefers to purchase a woman rather than date her. "How long would I have to—"

"A month," Gabriel says, his eyes a bright flame.

Scott is silent a moment. "That would bring in more money."

A month? God, what could a man do to me in a month? Even the thought of being with a stranger for a single night makes my stomach turn over. Bile rises in my throat. Would he want to sleep with me every day? More than that?

"What if—" I swallowed hard. "What if he hurts me?"

Scott shrugged. "It always hurts the first time. So I've heard."

I always imagined that I would have sex with my husband, that he would take care to make it easier for me. A man who paid for the privilege would have no reason to restrain himself. "I mean worse than that. You know…kinky stuff."

"Kinky stuff," Gabriel says, the corner of his mouth turned up. "What do you know about kinky stuff?"

My face feels hot. "I've seen the movie, okay? I know about things."

That's a lie. I squirmed through the movie, lips parted in shock. How did people think of this stuff? Why would any girl like it? And I'm not just a random face in this city. My picture has appeared in the society papers. People know my father. Maybe some of the men were cheated by him, just like Gabriel. Would they want to hurt me in revenge?

"Tell me what you know," Gabriel says.

The words are mocking, but something sparks inside me. "I know that some men like to hurt women. I know it makes them feel big and strong to hurt someone weaker."

"And are you weak, little virgin?"

No, I want to say. Except I've lost everything in the past two months. My life, my school. My friends. I'm a shadow of my former self. *Little virgin* makes me fight back, though. Gabriel makes me fight back. "I'm doing what I have to do. Is that weak?"

His gaze flickers over my body, the yellow of his eyes brighter in the lamp's glow. When he meets my eyes, there's a begrudging respect. "Scott will screen the men who get invited."

"Naturally," Scott says. "I'm not promising these men won't want kinky shit, but they'll respect reasonable boundaries."

That sounds a little vague—what qualifies as reasonable? But I would be stepping into their world, one with thorns and dark shadows. It would be dangerous.

It would be immoral. Daddy taught me to protect myself, but then he failed to protect me. I don't know what to believe anymore. "I don't—I don't know if I can do this."

Scott waves a hand as if it doesn't matter to him. Maybe it doesn't. "Go home, think it over. Come back tomorrow if you want to do it."

I take a step back, relieved to be dismissed. The thought of making a decision hurts my heart, but at least I have a reprieve.

"Oh, and Avery," Scott says thoughtfully. "If you do come back, bring some lingerie. We'll want to get some pictures circulating to generate interest."

I imagine myself undressed down to my bra, my underwear. More exposed than I am now. And photographs would last forever. That would only be the beginning, because when a man purchased my virginity, he could see every part of me. Touch every inch of my skin. Invade every place in my body. My eyes turn hot with tears. All I can manage is a curt nod, and then I'm practically running from the room.

I'm already in the hallway when I feel a hand on my wrist. Something inside me snaps, and I turn back with a cry of anger, of grief. Of defeat. I strike out with an open palm, trying to hit him, *hurt* him.

Gabriel subdues me with another hand on my wrist.

One step forward and he backs me into the wall. The rich wood paneling is cool through the cloth of my shirt. His body radiates heat at my front. I shrink against the unforgiving wall as if I can get away from him. He closes the space until we're a breath away.

"I was going to say you forgot your coat," he murmurs.

Then I see my trench coat draped over his arm. He's doing something nice, and I just freaked out at him. God, I'm so messed up inside—fear and shame churning in my stomach. "I'm sorry."

"You're right to fight me. I'm not a nice man."

And he was the one to suggest the auction. His hands are still holding my wrists against the wall, and I realize how exposed I am. "Are you going to let me go?"

His lips brush my temple. "Soon, little virgin."

"Don't call me that." My voice trembles only a little, revealing the turmoil inside me.

"What else should I call you? Princess? Darling?"

"You could call me by my name."

He dips his head, his mouth right by my ear, his voice just a breath. "There's only one thing I'm going to call you. *Mine.*"

The possession in his voice makes me shiver. "Never."

But a little voice inside my head says, *Not yet.*

He steps back with a quiet laugh. "You can run away, little virgin. But you'll come back."

I'm very afraid he's right.

CHAPTER TWO

THERE USED TO be gardeners working outside and the part-time chef in the kitchen. Maids working under the direction of the housekeeper. Ten thousand square feet of French architectural splendor doesn't tend itself.

When the scandal hit, things got even louder.

The phone rang constantly with Daddy's lawyers and business partners. The long street leading up to the cobblestone driveway became a gauntlet, teeming with reporters. There was even a protest once, with posters that read *Clean Up Corruption* and *Get Out of Tanglewood*.

Once-rounded bushes have grown wild, casting jagged shadows on empty pavement.

No one greets me as I walk through the front door. I follow the faint hum of machinery down the hallway and into my father's bedroom, where a hospital bed has replaced the crackled leather chairs in front of the fireplace.

Rosita looks up from her book with worry.

"How was it?"

"Oh, it was fine." I told her I had a meeting with some businesspeople.

She doesn't know the specifics, but she knows we're desperate for money. The empty rooms where oriental rugs and antique furniture used to sit are proof enough. I've sold everything, scraping every last penny from my late mother's loving decorating. Only my father's bedroom remains untouched—except for the IV drip and health monitors that help keep him alive.

I touch my father's hand, the skin papery. "Did he wake up?"

She glances at my father's resting face, her expression sad. "He had a few minutes of awareness soon after you left, but the drugs put him to sleep again."

Sadness is better than wariness, and definitely better than hatred, the way most of his former staff looked at him during those dark days. He had given them each a small severance package, which was nullified by the court once reparations were ordered. Millions of dollars of reparations depleted every one of his accounts.

And then he'd been attacked, beaten nearly to death.

I know on some level he deserved those

things. The censure, the debt. Maybe even the beating, by some morality standards. But it's hard to believe that when I see him struggling to breathe.

I dig through my purse for the bills tucked inside.

Rosita puts her hand over mine. "No, Miss Avery. It's not necessary."

It's easier to force a smile now that I've had practice. "It *is* necessary. And it's fine. Don't worry about me."

She shakes her head, dark eyes mournful. "I'm not blind." A pointed glance at my body. "I see how skinny you've gotten."

I cast a worried look at my father, but he's still asleep. "Please."

"No, I can't take your money." She hesitates. "But I can't watch your father either."

I open my mouth, but my pleas catch in my throat. How can I ask her to come back? She's the only one of our former staff to come at all. And she's right that I don't have the money to keep paying her. It's not her fault I'm running out of options.

"Okay," I say, my voice breaking.

"Your mother—" She makes a soft sound. "She would have been heartbroken to see this."

I know that, and it's the only solace I have in her death. She never had to see my father's fall from grace. She never had to see her little girl turned into a whore. "I miss her."

Rosita's gaze darts to my father, almost furtive. "She was loyal," she whispers. "Like you."

I nod because it isn't a secret. Everyone knew she was a doting wife and mother. A true society maven, friends with everybody and the picture of grace. I always dreamed of being like her one day, but I know that with the visit I made earlier, my life will be irrevocably changed.

"Be careful," Rosita finally adds with a pat to my hand. She takes one final glance at my father. "Mr. Moore is waiting in the back parlor."

My heart thuds.

Uncle Landon has been my father's friend and financial advisor for years. They played golf and the stock market. But even as close as he was, he never would have been invited to the back parlor. That was only for family, which is why the lumpy, comfortable couch wasn't worth anything.

I paste on an expression of nonchalance. "I'll speak to him when I'm done here."

Without another word, Rosita shows herself out. Steady beeps fill the space she left behind, clinical reminders of my father's tenuous hold on life.

Swallowing hard, I take his hand. This hand rocked me to sleep and tossed a softball. Now it seems cold and frail. I can feel every vein beneath the paper skin.

Tears rise up, but I fight them back. "Oh, Daddy."

I really need my biggest supporter right now. I need someone to tell me everything will be all right. There's no one left to do that. The only thing that will help now is a phone call from one of the city's crime lords. A rich man with money enough to buy a woman for the night.

His eyelids are shot through with blue-green veins. They open slowly, revealing the flat gaze he's had ever since the conviction. "Avery?"

"I'm here. Do you need anything? Are you hungry?"

He closes his eyes again. "I'm tired."

He's asleep most of the time. "I know, Daddy."

"You're a good girl," he says faintly, his eyelids fluttering.

My throat feels thick. "Thank you," I whisper.

"My little jumping jack."

His voice fades to nothing by the end, but I know what he said. He used to call me that when

I was little, boundless as little girls can be. He taught me chess to help me focus. And then he found time to play a game with me every week, no matter what. He worked nights and weekends, but he always made time to sit across the chessboard from me.

In the beeping quiet that follows, I know he's asleep again. I only get a few minutes with him a day. The rest of the time the medicine keeps him under, but without it he's in intense pain. He has always been a man of vitality, of action. Multiple broken bones and a harrowing night in the dark alley where they left him aged him twenty years. This is all he has left—the security of this room and the pain medicine. I can't take those away.

"Everything will be okay," I say out loud because I have to believe that. I have to believe that I'm doing this for a reason. Have to believe that it will be enough.

There's no one left to save us except me.

CHAPTER THREE

I HAVE THREE memories of my mother, and one of them takes place in the back parlor. She was a beautiful debutante, the perfect society wife. Only in the privacy of the back parlor did she ever sit on the floor to play Candy Land with me.

My footsteps echo in the hallway, made empty by my desperate need for money. Darkened rectangles decorate the wooden floor, patches where a rug or piece of furniture sat for a decade or two. Between the sale of our furniture and cashing in my college fund, I've kept us afloat for another month, but that will run out soon. The nurse who visits my father once a day, the doctor who replenishes his supply of pain medication. They all want money, both for their expertise and to keep their stories out of the city's gossip chain. What's left of my father's dignity is worth that much.

The door to the back parlor is open. Landon Moore sits on the lumpy couch, his vest impeccable, one oxford-clad foot slung over his leg. He has a full head of silver hair, a beard and mustache, and striking blue eyes. He reminds me of those old English gentlemen, minus the accent.

Part of me hates that he's encroached on the only thing I have left of my father. The practical part of me knows there aren't any other sofas in the house. No furniture. There's nothing left. Panic rises in my chest.

He's here to help you, I remind myself.

"Uncle Landon," I manage. "It's so good to see you."

He stands, his expression somber. "My dear girl. What a trying time this must be for you."

For reasons I can't explain, my lower lip trembles. His sympathy is harder to bear than the challenge in Gabriel Miller's chiseled face. I can't afford to feel sorry for myself. I can't afford to break down, not when I don't know if I'd be able to put myself back together again.

"I'm fine," I assure him. "You don't have to worry about me."

"Oh but I do, especially with your father out of commission. How is his health?"

His pallid skin, his weakened movements. The excruciating pain I can see in his eyes between doses. "He's improving every day. I'm just so grateful that he's healing."

"Good, good." He gestures to the sofa—my mother's sofa. "Come sit down with me. I must speak with you."

The front parlor was carefully constructed to provide decorum, to allow space. I could have sat in the beautiful Scottish armchairs with a small oak table between us. I could have maintained the smile on my face.

But the back parlor is made for comfort. For intimacy. And when I sit down, the cushions tilt sideways, sliding me closer to his body. He doesn't move away. Instead his hand lands on my knee with a squeeze. Every muscle freezes as I stare at the faint age spots on his skin, unable to comprehend what's happening, unwilling to think about why he's touching me like this.

"My dear, we need to discuss your future. We need to discuss the house."

"The house—" My voice cracks, and I take a deep breath. This isn't my house. It isn't even my father's. He built it for my mother. He gave it to her outright—a gift. And when she died it passed to me in trust. "You said we'd be able to keep the house."

"Yes, it's protected by the trust. But maintenance on an estate like this is, I'm sorry to say, a luxury you can no longer afford." He glances out the window with an expression of disapproval. The bushes had once been perfectly rounded. Green puffs of cotton candy, I once thought. Now they've grown unruly, jagged branches covering the window.

The house isn't luxury. It's the only thing I have left. I can't lose the house. It would break my father to find out how far we've fallen. It would break *me*.

"I had hoped to keep Daddy here. It's important."

Landon's face turns faintly pitying. "Unfortunately the real estate taxes are due soon. We haven't been paying into escrow for years, as the total would be easily covered by your family's accounts. But with the recent restitution payments..."

My mouth turns metallic with fear. "How much are the taxes?"

He reaches down to his leather folio and pulls out a folded paper. I take it with trembling hands, shaking hard enough to blur the numbers. When they finally come into focus, my breath expels completely. "Oh God."

"Yes," he agrees. "It was laudable to try and keep your father here, but I'm afraid it's quite impossible. I've already been in touch with a realtor and explained the need for a fast sale."

He goes on about the details of selling the house, but all I can hear are my father's faint words. *You're a good girl.* For so many years he took care of me. It's my turn to protect him.

"Wait," I say.

Landon's expression softens, the lines of his face relaxing. "I know how hard this must be for you. That's why I wanted to speak to you about a proposition."

"Something to save the house?" Something to save my father.

"I'm afraid not," he says gently. "But you know that I care for you deeply. I have the utmost respect for you."

I blink, uncertain where he's going with this. "Of course, Uncle Landon. You've always been here for us. And you've been a huge help to me with the finances during this time."

He gives me a genial smile. "Good, good. And I hope you'll be amenable to what I'm about to propose."

I hold my breath. For some reason I feel wary. As much as Uncle Landon visited from time to time, even though he was always kind to me, something about him made me uncomfortable.

His hand takes mine, pulling it into his lap.

My stomach tightens in shock and silent denial.

"I have had the pleasure of watching you blossom into a beautiful young lady. Your grace and strength during your father's trial have been admirable. It would be my great honor to make you my wife."

The air seems to whoosh from the room, my lungs hard and hollow. "What?"

"I realize that I may not have been your first choice—"

"Uncle Landon. You're like family to me." And he's as old as my father. They went to school together. How can he even ask me this?

"We'll still be family, Avery. I'll take good care of you."

My blood runs cold as I consider the implications. Uncle Landon is definitely rich in his own right, through inheritance and from his work as a financial advisor to the city's wealthy. The thought of accepting his proposal makes my stomach clench, but I can't say no. "You would keep the house?" I ask cautiously, my voice tight.

He stands and crosses to the mantle, where family pictures crowd together. My mother's smiling face features prominently, my only method to remember her. He picks up a frame and touches the glass, almost a caress. "Do you know I met your mother first? Before Geoffrey had seen her."

I shiver. "My father said it was love at first sight."

"Yes," he says, with a dark note that I've never heard before. "She was a beautiful flower, and he picked her as soon as he saw her. He built this house as a shrine to her."

My breath catches. This is why he could never countenance moving, even with all the extra space. This house isn't only for my father. It's a living memorial to my mother.

"So you'll help me save it?" I ask almost desperately.

He looks at me sharply. "It wouldn't be appropriate." As if realizing the harshness of his tone, he gives me a smile. "And it would be wasteful. I have a very large home that would be quite lovely for you."

"But my father…"

"He's barely conscious," Landon says, his tone curt. "We'll make him quite comfortable in a room in our house. And we'll be able to hire a full-time nurse to care for him."

Part of me wants to demand to know why he

won't pay for the nurse already, considering how destitute we are. Isn't he best friends with my father? Except his expression doesn't look kind right now. He seems almost bitter. Jealous? Has he held on to resentment all these years for my mother choosing my dad?

And how creepy would it be to marry Uncle Landon? It would have been bad already—the huge age difference, the fact that he watched me grow up. But knowing I'm a replacement to my mother?

"I can't," I whisper.

He returns to the couch, standing beside me, looking down. He runs a finger across my cheek, making goose bumps rise across my skin. "You've always been a smart girl. Surely you must see there's no other choice."

Gazing up at him, Gabriel's golden eyes flash in my mind. Isn't this the safer choice? I've known Uncle Landon my entire life. I would be able to live comfortably, in the style I am accustomed to. My father's medical bills would be taken care of.

Some small, broken part of me wants to give myself over to this, to let someone else fix everything. I've had to be strong for so long, watching my life crumble before me. The thought of lying beneath Uncle Landon's body repulses me, but some stranger at an auction probably wouldn't be better.

His thumb brushes across my lips, and everything in me recoils. I hold myself very still, even my breath bated. This is the test, I realize. To see whether I can stand his touch.

"So much like her," he murmurs, and I know he means my mother. "At the same age I met her."

A shudder rushes through me. "No," I whisper.

It's too much knowing he's imagining my mother. It's too much thinking of him like family.

"Avery, I'm trying to help you."

"I have another plan," I say with that falling sensation again. I'm tumbling, turning. Uncle Landon is my only hope of ground, but somehow I've decided to jump.

"What plan?"

"I'm going to get a loan from Damon Scott."

Landon pulls back in surprise. "The loan shark?"

"He's a businessman. He's going to lend me enough for the real estate taxes. And the nurse. I'll be able to keep the house." I'm lying out of desperation right now, pretending it will be a loan instead of an auction, praying it will be enough money.

"That much money," Landon says slowly. "Are you sure he doesn't want some-thing…unsavory from you?"

That's what you want from me. I press my lips together, praying for the strength to go through with it. I know the mercy that Uncle Landon is offering me. Not only would he support me, but his standing in the community might be enough to save me in the eyes of society.

But I would be married to him for the rest of my life. Considering he's thirty years older than me, more likely the rest of *his* life. It's still a long time.

Far longer than a month.

Selling my virginity to a stranger would be horrifying, but it would only last for a month. I could survive that. And maybe, with time and with luck, I would almost forget what had happened. Uncle Landon would save me, but the cost would be years.

"It's already agreed," I lie. "I'm going to re-turn tomorrow to finalize the contract."

"I must advise against this," he says. "The in-terest rates are no doubt outrageous, if not illegal. And how will you raise the funds to make payments?"

"Don't worry, Uncle Landon. I have it all worked out."

Because I won't be making payments, at least not with money. I'll be using my body to pay for those taxes, to pay for the nurse. Even as I make the decision, I'm torn with regret and fear. Should I have said yes to Uncle Landon? I can't imagine spreading my legs for him. Then again I can't imagine spreading my legs for a stranger.

CHAPTER FOUR

T HAT NIGHT I dream of a fire licking at my skin, and when I wake, I'm sweating in my sheets. My mattress is on the floor, the only thing remaining in the room after my Victorian bedroom set was sold through an antiques dealer. I don't want to dream anymore, so I get up and roam the halls. The moonlight slices through the heavy branches, drawing geometric patterns on the empty wooden floors.

I head downstairs and pour a glass of water. It slides down my throat, cool and centering. Whatever happens in that auction, I'll get through it. Only a month and then it will be over.

I'm making the right choice, aren't I?

A shadow through the window catches my eye, and my blood turns cold. It must be a wild branch from the bushes. This is what happens when they aren't trimmed. Still, I stand to the side, watching the window. Only darkness stares back at me.

I laugh uneasily. "You're paranoid, Avery."

Meeting with criminals must have made me suspicious.

Another shadow crosses the window. My heart leaps into my throat, thick and pulsing. Oh God. Did I see someone outside? My imagination turns wild—monsters and imaginary beings. Those myths from my books come to life.

More likely it would be a burglar who hasn't realized we lost everything of value.

Or maybe someone did know about our fall from grace—and that I would be alone and unprotected in the house. My blood runs cold. As Gabriel Miller pointed out, I have one thing left of value. My body. My virginity. Maybe the man outside wants that.

I step close to the window, trying to see outside. The moon hides behind a cloud, the ground lights obscured by overgrowth, leaving the lawn almost completely black.

Is someone hiding out there?

Are they picking the lock even while I stand here, defenseless?

My imagination's getting the better of me. No one would be out there. I have my entire life in safety. I hadn't realized that anyone would want to hurt us until the police called me. A dish washer found my father behind their restaurant.

They dumped his body there after beating him.

What if they've come back to finish the job?

Ice in my veins, I dash back up the stairs. My phone sits beside my mattress. I grab it and start to dial the number for Uncle Landon. He's the only one in Tanglewood who still speaks to me.

Then I remember the strange light in his eyes when he talked about my mother.

The longing was surprising enough, but there was something darker underneath. Resentment. Maybe anger.

Instead I find myself dialing my friend Harper. I glance at the time just as she picks up. After two in the morning. No doubt she's still awake. I don't know when she sleeps. She's the pale blonde co-ed to my girl next door, the marble statue to my straw man. The real deal.

"Avery!" she says, breathless. "Jesus God, it's like you fell off the face of the planet."

I know from the southern drawl in her voice that she's very drunk. A faint beat in the background underscores her words, reminding me of late-night study sessions and frat parties at the nearby university. That should be my life right now.

Instead I'm huddling against the wall in a dark, empty house. "I'm sorry I didn't call sooner, but I'm kind of freaked out."

"I'm freaking out," she says, laughing. "Are you coming back now? I've missed you!"

There's a sound from outside—a scratch. My breathing speeds up. "I think someone's outside."

The sound of shuffling and the slam of a door come over the line. Immediately the volume drops. "Wait, what's going on?" she says, sounding more sober. "Are you okay?"

I was too ashamed of my fall from grace to call Harper with a play-by-play of Daddy's trial. She left me a couple voicemails, but how could I explain that I was never going back to school? I could barely even admit the truth to myself. The entire life I had when I knew her is gone now.

"I don't know," I whisper, resting my back against the wall beside the window. "I might be losing my mind."

One man offered to sell my virginity, another proposed marriage, all in the same day. It was enough to make a girl go crazy. Yes, I'd gone round the bend. I had to pray that's the cause of those shadows and noises.

"Break it down for me," she says. "You said you're at home. Your dad's house, right?"

She knows about the charges he faced. I admitted that much when I left school last semester. She may have even read about the convictions if she followed the trial. But my father's beating isn't public knowledge. "He's sick," I say, which is an understatement. "And it's just the two of us. I thought I saw something outside but...I don't know for sure."

"Can you call the cops?"

We aren't exactly on the cops' favored list after my dad was indicted on multiple counts of fraud and embezzlement. The last thing I want to do is call them only to find a racoon outside. They would probably arrest me for making a false emergency call. And then who would take care of Daddy?

"I guess I'd like to know there's something really out there before I call. I've had kind of a wild day, so maybe I'm just imagining things."

"Okay, well, obviously I want to hear about this wild day, but can't you call your dad's people? Didn't he have some kind of security detail?"

There were always men trailing us when we went to the zoo or the museum. They went out of their way to be unobtrusive, but I thought it was normal. Only when I got older did I realize how strange it was. My dad said it was just a precaution, something to keep us safe after my mother died in a drunk-driving accident.

Then the scandal hit.

Daddy's business lost all its contracts even before he was found guilty. And he couldn't afford the security guards when he needed them most. Couldn't afford them when he most needed protection.

"We don't have them anymore. After the court cases—" I remember the horror of seeing my dad in the hospital, half his face covered in bruises, the other half in bandages. It was worse when the doctors explained that he would probably never walk again. "Things have been bad."

She makes a sympathetic sound. "You should have called me."

"I know. I was just…embarrassed. Maybe a little bit in denial."

"Okay, look. Are the floodlights on? Can you turn something on outside to see better?"

"This is why I called you." I'm so flustered by Uncle Landon that I can't even think. No, that's not true. It's Gabriel who's kept me up late, tossing and turning in bed. "There have to be lights somewhere."

I never had occasion to use them, but I go into the mud room and find a long row of lights.

Already I feel less shaky from hearing Harper's familiar voice. Both of us made our way in the world like American princesses, unafraid and confident of our acceptance. Some of that old comfort winds its way to me across the phone line.

"Turning on the lights," I tell her, laying my palm sideways to flip them all up at once.

Blinding white lights flood the lawn like an airplane strip. And that's when I see the man working at the electricity box, something glinting in his hand. Is he cutting the power? Oh God. My pulse races as I stand rooted to the tile floor.

"Avery? Avery!" Harper's voice comes to me as if from far away.

"Someone's here," I say faintly.

The man stumbles back, surprised by the sudden lights. He's wearing a black hooded jacket and dark jeans. I can't see his face.

"Avery, do you hear me? Go into your bedroom and lock the door."

My feet carry me—not to my bedroom, but to my father's. I lock the door and sink to the floor, listening to Harper borrow a friend's phone and call the cops. She talks to me through the next few minutes, promising me that everything will be okay.

I know she's wrong. Even if I make it through tonight, my life is over.

My dad doesn't wake up, the steady beeps telling me he's fine.

The cops show up with a loud bang on the door. They explore the large grounds, but there's no sign of an intruder. Their expressions are disbelieving when I describe what I saw, but it doesn't matter. I know now that we aren't safe here. We won't be safe anywhere. Not without money.

CHAPTER FIVE

THE THING ABOUT being a virgin is that I don't really have any sexy lingerie. No one has ever seen my underwear except other girls in the gym changing room. I wear sturdy skin-toned bras and cute underwear with pink doughnuts and blue butterflies on them. Nothing with lace or silk.

I stare at the slim contents of my underwear drawer without inspiration as sunlight streams through the window. Last night the lawn seemed ominous, concealing intruders in its shadows. In the daylight it seems like the same cheery place I played as a child. It's almost enough to make me forget the intruder last night, except that I found the little metal clasp on the electrical box broken. The cops assure me that the lock can get broken in a bad storm, but I know what I saw.

There's only one way to make sure we're safe here.

In the end it's too late to get a fancy bra-and-panty set. Besides, my credit card would get declined. I pull on a plain white T-shirt bra and white panties with a pretty scalloped edge.

If they want a virgin, then they can damn well deal with my underwear.

I have a few fancy dresses left from my days attending opening galas and evening operas, ones I couldn't sell because they were ripped or too old. But I can't quite bring myself to dress in a daring red or mysterious black. These are dresses I wore on Justin's arm, the toast of society. That girl doesn't exist anymore.

Instead I put on a white sundress. At least it hugs my curves.

I find sandals and a clutch to match, pretending I'm getting ready for brunch with friends.

There will be no more brunches. Maybe no more friends. And I won't see Justin ever again. A pang in my chest reminds me that I love him—that I love a man who saw me as a stepping stone.

The Den looks different today, more like one of the historic buildings dotting Tanglewood's downtown. There are offices and stores bustling with people at two in the afternoon.

Maybe I should have waited until tonight.

A knock on the brass ring in a lion's mouth goes unanswered.

I need to do this before I lose my nerve. I knock harder this time, almost hurting my knuckles against the thick wood. Why aren't they answering? Maybe they aren't here, but I can't turn back now. I'm too deep into this.

Some impulse puts my hand on the door-knob. It turns.

Why isn't the door locked? Unease moves through my stomach. I expected to find Gabriel opening the door like he did last night. He scared me then, but for some reason I miss him now.

I wander down the hallway, into the large room filled with plush leather armchairs and tables that have been cleared of ashtrays and half-filled glasses. Only smooth surfaces remain, gleaming in the faint light. I take a step back, another—backing out of a room I shouldn't be in.

A sound comes to me faintly, and I whirl. The wide hallway is empty.

There's a door at the end of the hall, and it draws me closer with strange magnetism. My feet move on their own, bringing me to the forbidden. I shouldn't even be in the Den, much less wander-ing the hallways alone. My curiosity has always gotten me into trouble, but before I had the security of my family name. Now I'm falling without a net.

The door opens to a set of dark wooden stairs. Servants' quarters, I realize. These old houses were divided by class. The steps lead up to another door, no place to wait except two steps down. My knock echoes through the dim hallway, overloud and startling even though I made the sound.

I chance a look down the stairs, at the shadowed landing below, darkness impenetrable. Dizzy waves rush over me. I'm in one of those twisting sketches with stairs that turn into themselves, a never-ending maze. I'll never find my way back.

The door swings open, and then a large body slams into mine—as hard and solid as the stairs beneath my feet. I lose my grip on the rail and fall backward, world upside down. *Oh God, I'm falling.*

I twist in the air, all sense of balance lost, no ground to fall back on. Firm hands grasp my arms, almost bruising. They haul me upright, toes brushing the steps, gaze snapping to fierce eyes and a snarl.

Wild. That's all I can think of the man holding me up. Heavy eyebrows slant over copper eyes, the pupils large enough to make him almost feral. This close I can see his features better, lit by the overhead light instead of the dim room downstairs. His nose and mouth are crude, etched from stone instead of flesh. The whole effect is made more sinister by the faint slash through his cheek and upper lip, a scar so deep and so old it's a part of his features now, a thin sliver of water through a canyon wall.

"Whoa," comes his low voice, like I'm the animal. Like I need settling.

Too late I hear the soft keening sound I'm making. I fall silent. "I'm sorry."

He drags me inside, setting me down on the wooden floor with a hollow clack of my sandals. My ankles turn, topsy turvy. He frowns down at the white leather straps of my sandals as if they don't belong—and God, he's right. They're from another life. Another girl, one who'd never step foot in a place like this.

Gabriel's voice cuts through the thick air. "Did I hurt you?"

I can still feel the imprint of his fingers on my arms, the solid muscles of his chest as he rammed into me. Hurt, yes. Pain like rays of sunlight through the cloudy numbness I've been living in.

"I'm fine." A lie.

Bronze eyes narrow, taking in the slim line of my dress, the designer clutch. I'm too broke to even afford a knock-off—how's that for irony?

"I'm ready for you."

I'm still falling. Catch me. But he isn't my white knight. No one's going to save me. "Ready?"

He makes a rough sound, maybe amusement. Maybe pleasure. "To take pictures."

My breath stutters. "You're going to take them?"

"There's a photographer. He's excellent. Damon would have been here as well to make sure he gets the right shots, to make sure you're...cooperative. But he has another engagement." His grin is almost feral. "I volunteered to stand in for him."

Pride feels heavy in my throat. "You enjoy seeing me fall."

Maybe I should have expected that, considering my father cheated him. But he already turned Daddy in to the authorities, his evidence the impetus for the indictment. I suppose for a man like him that wouldn't be enough. Had he been the one to send men to attack my father?

Had he sent men to my house last night?

Gabriel's voice is bland. "Maybe I just enjoy watching a beautiful woman."

With his wealth and his devastating looks, he could have any woman he wants. But after what he did to my father, he would never have me.

Unless he buys your virginity at the auction, a small voice taunts me.

He wouldn't do that, would he?

I glance back down the stairs as if I have a chance to escape. "The photographer's already setting up? How did you know I would come?"

"Desperate times."

The men of the Den control this city with wealth, influence. Power. "Familiar with desperate measures, are you?"

"They're my bread and butter."

"Drugs," I say, accusatory. "Guns?"

"Sex," he says, his voice mocking.

No, my hands aren't clean. But I still feel out of my depth. I may have benefited from my father's secret criminal deals, but I never knew about them. "Yes," I whisper.

"So innocent," he murmurs. "This is a whole new world for you, isn't it?"

He doesn't sound sympathetic. I'm a curiosity to him, something to bat around like a mouse between his claws. "You don't have to make me cooperate. I'm going through with it."

His smile is almost sad. "I know, little virgin. You don't have a choice."

With that he turns from me and leads the way

down a hall.

Dread clenches my stomach, but he's right. I don't have a choice.

Part of me wonders why they wouldn't take the pictures downstairs, with the beautiful crown molding and elaborate furniture. I find my answer as soon as I enter the small room. It might have been a bedroom for servants, two thin beds on either side, the ceiling slanted above us. The window is old enough to be made from warbled glass, lending a dreamy look to the light, almost as if we're underwater.

There are white photographer screens placed around the room that only seem to amplify the effect. On one side a man fiddles with a large camera on a tripod. He looks up when we come in, his bushy eyebrows rising. "This is the subject?"

I swallow hard, thrown by the lack of hello. I'm already an object to be photographed for auction, a chair or a rug. Not a person anymore.

"She'll take the dress off," Gabriel says.

My breath catches. "Do I really need to do that? I thought the sundress might be…"

"Provocative?" Gabriel offers blandly. "Perverse? Yes, but some of the men on the invite list can be rather…obvious. They would prefer to see skin."

"Right." I swallow hard. "It's just that I didn't have any...any sexy lingerie. Just my regular stuff."

"Your regular stuff?" Gabriel asks with a lift of his eyebrow. "Show me."

Only then do I realize I'll have to undress in front of two men, one I've just met. Only then do I realize that showing my regular underwear and bra is somehow more intimate than a matching lace set.

This is something I thought only my husband would ever see.

Shaking hands reach behind me to unzip the dress. The straps slide off my shoulders with the simple movement. I stand like that for a breathless, frozen moment, knowing there's no going back.

I don't even have to push the dress away from me. I let my hands fall to my sides, and the soft material falls down my body, a caress as solid as Gabriel's golden gaze.

"Jesus," the photographer mutters, staring at my plain white bra, the white panties.

I manage not to cringe. This isn't what a sexy woman would wear. This isn't going to earn anything at auction. "I'm sorry," I whisper miserably.

I've only just started this and I'm already failing.

"It's perfect," Gabriel says, sounding almost reverent. "You're perfect."

Goose bumps rise across my skin. It takes everything in me not to snatch my dress, not to run from the room. Maybe he does need to ensure my cooperation. I'm already trembling, and all they're doing is looking. How will I stand it when a strange man climbs on top of me?

I look away, at a point on the plain white-washed walls. "How should I stand?"

My voice is stiff, betraying my nerves.

Footsteps come closer, and I know without looking that it's Gabriel. It might be something about his gait, graceful and confident. More likely it's the way my body electrifies whenever he's near.

He touches my chin and turns my face to him. "I'll show you."

There's something almost encouraging in his eyes, a strange infusion of strength. I shouldn't trust it, shouldn't trust *him,* but I find myself standing straighter anyway. "Okay."

"We'll start with some shots from the front." He moves to stand behind me, brushing my hair over the tops of my breasts, arranging the heavy locks over my face. "The advance pictures will hide your face."

"They won't know who I am?" It's a small relief that there won't be half-naked pictures of me—identifiable pictures, including my face—circulating in the city.

"If they want to know who you are, they'll have to pay ten grand."

"Ten grand," I gasp, shame and elation warring within me. If enough people show up, I can pay the real estate tax bill. "How many men do you think will come?"

"Damon will keep the attendance fees."

Of course he will. He isn't hosting the auction out of the goodness of his heart. A perverse amusement rises in me, imagining this as a charity auction—my family's tattered dignity the cause. We could set up little cardboard boxes for quarters at gas stations. Maybe organize a bake sale. "And I'll get the amount that's bid?"

"Minus his percentage," Gabriel says smoothly.

"Hey," I say, half turning to face him. "I'm the one doing all the work."

"Never fear, little virgin. You'll make plenty selling your wares." He turns me to face the camera again, this time tipping my head forward so my hair creates a veil over my face.

His palms run down my arms, sending sparks of sensation over my skin. He nudges them forward, plumping my breasts. It's a strange position, almost like prayer.

"Stay," he murmurs, his breath soft against my neck.

Then he steps away, and the photographer starts clicking. My stomach turns over as I imagine strange old men looking at these pictures, evaluating my body, judging my monetary worth.

When the clicking stops, Gabriel steps forward and turns me sideways. He lifts my hands so that they rest on my head, elbows forward, revealing the shape of my breasts, my butt. Gabriel only touches me on my arms, and even then he's businesslike. Weirdly respectful, considering the situation. He could take the opportunity to feel me up. I couldn't stop him. Instead he gives my shoulder a reassuring squeeze before stepping back.

More clicking, some flashes from the equipment stationed around the room.

I close my eyes tight, waiting for it to be over.

"Hmm," Gabriel says, his voice coming from near the camera. Is he looking at the pictures through the lens? What does he see when he looks at me? "Let's try some with her facing away."

They must not be good. That's my only thought as I turn to face the wall like a child being punished. I'm so inherently unsexy that only a picture of my backside could possibly appeal to anyone. Panicked thoughts race through me, making me tremble, making me shake.

His hands land on my shoulders, and I suck in a ragged breath. "This isn't going to work," I whisper, half to him, half to myself. "I'll never be able to go through with it."

He speaks without turning me around, both of us facing the wall. "You said you're a virgin, but exactly how inexperienced are we talking?"

The most embarrassing part is that I don't know how to answer that question. Girls in my school whispered about what they did with their boyfriends. Lord knows Harper has told me some dirty things, but they almost felt like a made-up story to me. People don't really do those things to each other, do they?

I would find out soon enough. I'd experience them firsthand.

"I've done things," I say even though it feels like a lie.

"What kind of things?" he says, and I wonder

whether it's prurient interest or concern that compels him to ask. "Making out on the couch when Daddy isn't home? Letting a boy feel under your shirt?"

"No," I whisper.

"Have you ever been kissed?"

I manage to nod. That was as far as I let Justin go. He pushed me for more in the darkened back hallways at parties, in the empty storage rooms outside hotel ballrooms.

And I always told him no.

"What are you afraid of?" he murmurs.

The way he asks, I know he doesn't mean the auction. He's asking why I never let a boy go further with me. He's asking why I'm still a virgin.

Our position makes it feel more intimate, as if there isn't a stranger only a few feet behind us, as if I'm not being forced to do this. The wavy lighting adds to the effect, as if this is only in a dream. I can tell the truth because this isn't even real.

"Daddy caught me once," I say as if in a trance. "I was sleeping in on the weekend, or he thought I was. But I was actually touching myself."

"What did he say?"

"He told me it was wrong. He said that it wasn't ladylike, that that kind of behavior would disgrace our family name." The intense shame I felt then hits me like a blow to the stomach, almost doubling me over. It's only Gabriel's steady presence behind me that holds me up. He hardly touches me, only the lightest brush of his hands on my arms, but they might as well be made of iron.

"And then he was the one who disgraced your family name."

"He put chili juice on my fingers every night for a month."

The irony is enough to make me throw up. For years I resisted what the other girls were doing, refused what the boys wanted from me. The only boy willing to wait until marriage was Justin, and it turned out that was only because he viewed our relationship as a political stepping stone.

"Stay here, little virgin."

He moves away from me, and I feel his loss like a wintry wind. I'm alone, bereft.

The camera clicks behind me, invading my privacy, reminding me of just how public this will be. I can't even touch my body without feeling guilt, but some stranger will soon have the right.

"Look at me." Gabriel's voice comes to me from near the camera.

I turn to look at him over my shoulder. Most of my face is still hidden by my hair, but he can see more of me. Is my turmoil visible in my posture? Can they read the pain in my eyes? Everything that I believed was a lie, but the truth hurts enough that I want it back.

"Touch yourself," he says.

My heart stops, because if he wants me to do this for the camera, I'll falter. I'll fail.

"Tonight. When you're in bed, alone. In the dark. Lock the door if you need to. No one will walk in on you. Touch yourself and make yourself feel good. You remember how to do that, don't you?"

The memory comes like a tangible caress, a stroke on my private place. My lips part on a soft sigh. Heat suffuses my cheeks. I squeeze my legs together, seeking more.

The click of the camera captures my illicit pleasure.

"That's it," the photographer says.

Gabriel studies whatever is on the view screen, his expression enigmatic. "Yes. That's the one."

CHAPTER SIX

BOTH MEN STEP outside to let me dress. It only takes a moment to slip my sundress over my head. I use the privacy to gather my composure. I can't believe I told Gabriel about that time with my dad.

And then he was the one who disgraced your family name.

Maybe it's crazy to stand by my father, but I'm all he has left. Bedridden, barely able to breathe. He raised me from the moment my mother died. If I were to abandon him, he'd die. Whether from his injuries or from men coming to finish the job. I put my hands to my cheeks, feeling lingering heat.

How will I face Gabriel Miller now that he knows my secrets?

Except I need to confront him to find out if he sent the men to my house yesterday. Part of me wants to believe that he wouldn't do that, but the timing is too coincidental. And he has the most motive to want my father dead.

Taking a deep breath, I open the door and step into the small hallway.

It's darker than I remember, darker than it was in the dreamlike bedroom, and I blink while my eyes adjust. I realize that someone has turned off the overhead light in the hall. And I'm not alone.

"Gabriel?" I say, my voice wavering slightly.

A low laugh fills the space, darker and with more grit than I expect. "He went downstairs," says an unfamiliar voice.

Fear spikes in my chest. "Oh. I'll go look for him."

"You should be running the other way."

I take a step toward the stairs, backing away. I know that Gabriel isn't safe. He has a reason to hurt me. But something about this man makes my blood turn to ice.

"I'll keep that in mind," I say, squinting to make out his features. All I can see is pale hair and pale eyes.

"In fact, you ought to be running far away. The James family isn't welcome in this city anymore. Or haven't you figured that out yet?"

Old loyalty sparks anger inside me. "I'm very aware of my family's standing in Tanglewood.

That's the reason I'm in this mess."

"Sex for money. I guess it's more honest work than your daddy did, but just as dirty."

I flinch in the darkness. Something in his voice sounds personal. "What do you know about what my daddy did?"

"Your father stole from Gabriel Miller, and nobody gets away with that. That's why he got knocked down. But Gabriel wasn't the only person he stole from."

And all those men would want to hurt my dad. "He isn't stealing from anyone anymore."

In the shadows I see a broad shoulder shrug. "Doesn't make people whole again, does it? Though I suppose if they had you in their beds, taking the money out on your skin, that might make them feel better."

Fear is a finger down my spine, making my whole body shudder. I spin away from him and fly down the wooden stairs, heart pounding wildly. Part of me expects him to follow, and I speed up in anticipation of a hand on my shoulder, a fist in my hair.

Then I'm in the wide foyer, warmly lit by lamps along the wall. *Safe.*

Except safety is only an illusion when I'm in the Den.

Gabriel waits for me in the cozy leather chair where Damon was sitting last time. There's a glass in his hand, half-full, and he watches me with an unreadable expression.

I meant to question him carefully, but all my caution has evaporated. "Did you send someone to my house last night?"

For a moment he's so still I think he hasn't heard me. Then he leans forward, setting the glass on the table. "Someone came to your house?"

Of course a man like him would be an accomplished liar. I have to be smarter than him. Except if he did send someone, what could I do about it? The police were useless. "I surprised him when he was tampering with my electrical box. He left before the police came. Was it you?"

He speaks slowly, as if wondering the answer himself. "Why would I tamper with your electrical box?"

The shame of undressing upstairs mixes with my fear of the unnamed man. Something inside me snaps, pooling tears in my eyes. "To scare me. To hurt me. For the same reason you turned my father in."

His expression darkens. "Your father stole from me."

"Did you get your money back?" I ask tightly.

"No, but it wasn't about that. I made an example out of him."

My heart squeezes as I remember my dad's rasping breath. "Right, except I'm the one giving up my friends, my future. I'm the one who's going to be auctioned off."

He frowns. "Did you get a look at the man's face?"

"He was wearing a hoodie." I did get a feel for his build, his gait. Could he have been Gabriel Miller? Could he have been the man upstairs? Even if he wasn't either of them, he could have been sent by them.

"Someone will guard the house tonight," he says casually as if I should take his innocence for granted. He's anything but innocent. "If he comes back, we'll catch him."

My eyes narrow. "Why would you do that for me?"

One dark eyebrow rises. "Damon is going to make a lot of money on your auction. He's going to want to protect his investment."

Of course. I have become a product. My security would be a safe around a diamond, meant to keep me away from other men. Only, the most dangerous men in the city have the combination. It isn't protection at all. It's a cage.

I leave without another word, stomach tight until I'm back in my house with the door locked. I take a shower, trying to wash away the shame of their gazes on my skin, the light touch of Gabriel's hands on my arms. No matter how hard I scrub, I can still feel him.

CHAPTER SEVEN

OVER THE WEEKS since my father came home from the hospital, I've fallen into a routine. I check my father's vitals in the morning and change his bedding, which he mostly sleeps through. Then at midday I come and bring him lunch. That's the best chance I have to catch him awake. He can only handle liquids—warm soup and cold pudding. Sometimes he can stomach a few bites.

At school my major was classical studies with a focus on ancient mythology. It was fascinating for me, but far more suited for the wife of a senator than someone who had to measure medicine and administer shots.

By the time I fall onto my mattress every night, my muscles are sore. My body is tired, but my mind remains stubbornly awake—running over every weekly chess game of my childhood, every hour of the trial, every excruciating second of the breakup with Justin.

Since I met Gabriel yesterday, I have something new to obsess about.

After dressing in panties and a cami, my usual sleep clothes, I glance outside the window. A gleaming black SUV sits on the curb in plain sight. My heart lurches. What if someone's come back? Except the car isn't hidden at all. And when I squint, I can make out the silhouette of a man inside.

Damon Scott must have sent him.

He's going to want to protect his investment.

I close my eyes and take a deep breath.

From across the room my phone blinks a green light at me. A voicemail. I reach for it with shaking fingers, not sure whether I want to hear from Damon. He couldn't have set up the auction that quickly, could he? I press the phone to my ear.

My blood goes cold for a different reason as I hear Landon Moore's voice.

"My dear Avery. I understand that you were shocked by my proposal. I realize now that you need time to process the change. I was surprised to discover that you had grown into such a beautiful young woman. I confess that I had considered our union before these unfortunate events, but I feared that you would never see me as more than your dear Uncle Landon. I can be patient during this difficult time and trust that you'll make the right decision."

My dinner threatens to come up, and I toss the phone across the bare wood floors. It's harder to bear his patience because I don't know if I'm making the right choice. I can't bring myself to accept him, to bind myself to him for life, even though that might make things easier for me.

I also can't bring myself to give up this house, the only remnant of my mother.

What would she tell me to do if she were here?

How would my life have been different if she were alive? I would have had someone to teach me about my body. About sex. I would have had someone to explain how my period works instead of the school nurse. I would have had someone to tell me about sex instead of chili juice on my fingers.

Touch yourself.

Gabriel's words come back to me in a sensual rush, my heart pounding.

He didn't mean it, did he? It's just some stupid, taunting thing he said to get the right picture. And if he did mean it, it's not like I have to listen to him. He's a horrible man.

Except I find myself reaching for the sheet even though it's a warm night. I'm alone in the house with the doors locked. There's a man outside watching to make sure no one tampers with the electricity again. My dad is asleep, attached to his hospital bed, unable to walk in on me if he woke up.

When you're in bed, alone. In the dark. Lock the door if you need to.

Still I pull the sheet over my body. The thin layer of fabric is my shield from the fear, from the shame that burns inside me. I want to pretend I never heard his words, to act like they don't matter.

No one will walk in on you.

Except if I can't even touch myself, how can I let some man touch me? If I have never had an orgasm, how can I expect some stranger to give me one? He might not give me pleasure, but it would be even worse if he did. I imagine being helpless in the arms of some cold, distant man.

He would own me. I can't give someone that power over me, not even for money.

I start by touching my breasts because that feels less scary. They're warm and firm, my nipples already hard from thinking about this. I close my eyes while my fingers toy with my nipples. They are little zings of pleasure, in my breasts, in my core, but not enough. Not enough to come.

Touch yourself and make yourself feel good. You remember how to do that, don't you?

I never made myself come, but I remember where I liked to rub my body. My palms run across my stomach, down to my panties. I spread my legs, taking deep breaths. The conditioning runs deep with me. There's already a faint burn, the long-ago memory of chili juice when I tested it against my sex.

For a horrible moment I hear my father's voice telling me that I'm dirty, that I'm a disgrace. And I realize that it's not just about some strange man owning me. My father owns me. All these years he's kept me from my own body.

So is Gabriel giving it back? Or is he taking the reins?

I imagine his golden eyes watching me, knowing and sure. My inner muscles clench in response. There's something dangerous about him. It's not only what he did to my family, not only the harm to my father. There's a threat inherent in him, like a lion stalking his prey. It's mesmerizing even while it terrifies me.

There's an ache, a feeling of tightness whenever I think about him. The dark hair long enough to curl at the ends. The jaw shadowed with stubble. The broad shoulders that suit a man of power. My body responds even if my heart shrinks in fear. It's sickening, but God, so damned welcome. I'm tired of clenching my hands against my impulses, so tired of being ashamed.

My fingers are clumsy as they roam my sex, remembering where to stroke myself, finding the place where a touch feels too rough. I have to circle around it, and a sort of haze lowers over my mind.

Pleasure laps at my skin like gentle waves against the shore. I could do this forever, my finger slowly moving, my hips nudging up slightly. There's no urgency. Only peace.

Then that strange man's voice rises, unbidden, from the shadows of my mind.

I suppose if they had you in their beds, taking the money out on your skin, that might make them feel better. It should scare me, but in this sex-drowsed state, with Gabriel fresh in my mind, something else happens. Desire pulses through my body, a drop of liquid lust tickling my skin on its way down.

It's not hard to imagine him doing something

daring. Would he hurt me?

A man like Gabriel Miller would never be gentle. Even his words are sharp. They cut me, leaving my pride in shards at his feet. His eyes slice to the core of me. What would his hands do? His mouth? *His cock?*

Pressure builds in my sex, and I circle faster and faster. Harder, abusing the small nub of nerves until my body shudders and shakes, mouth open in a silent scream. Liquid spills over my fingers, dampening the fabric of my panties as my sex pulses for eternity.

In the aftermath my muscles feel stiff. Pulling my wet fingers up makes me blush. I rub them furtively on the sheets as if I'll get caught with them, shiny and sex smelling in the dark.

"What are you doing to me?" I whisper to the hollow room.

I don't know whether I'm talking to Gabriel or my father. I might as well be asking the question to myself. How could I climax thinking of Gabriel Miller? How could I come imagining being hurt?

CHAPTER EIGHT

THE NEXT MORNING I wake up to ringing of the doorbell. My heart leaps to my throat as I pull on a pair of jeans over my panties and tank top. In the bright light of day I'm more worried about some overzealous bill collector than a hooded man. Real estate bills with arms and legs, standing as tall as a skyscraper, have invaded my dreams. I'm half expecting us to be evicted for some unknown bill before we even get to the auction.

I open the door to a bright-eyed Harper, who's holding up two steaming cups of coffee. "Good morning, sleepyhead!"

Embarrassment burns my throat like acid. She would have already seen the overgrown state of the yard. As soon as she comes inside, she'll see the empty rooms where furniture used to be.

Even knowing she'll find out the truth, I can't help my joy at seeing her. I've been desperately alone since I came back from college. One by one all Tanglewood friends abandoned me.

I throw my arms around her neck, surprising us both by bursting into tears. "Oh my God, I'm so sorry."

She squeezes me back. "Oh, Avery. Tell me everything."

Over her shoulder I spot a glossy black car with a man leaning against it, a cigarette in his mouth. He notices me looking and gives me a mock salute.

A shiver runs through me. "Let's go inside."

Sitting on the floor in the empty living room, sipping our soy chai lattes, I tell her about the horrible court dates, where reporters hounded us on the way up and down the marble steps. I tell her about the convictions, how my father seemed to age ten years overnight as the *guilty* verdicts rang out. And I tell her about the horrible night I got a phone call from the police telling me my father was in the hospital.

Harper's brown eyes fill with tears. "Christ, Avery. How could you try and keep all this to yourself? You're too strong for your own good."

It all felt like a nightmare, but when I speak the words aloud, they become real. "I guess I was just taking it one day at a time. And for a while Daddy tried to keep a brave face, telling me that he'd fix everything. But they were just words. And after the attack…the doctors say he'll never really recover."

"You aren't coming back to school," she says, and it isn't a question.

I shake my head. "There's no way. Maybe someday in the future I can think about college again, but right now I have to focus on Daddy. He needs me."

She looks down, fiddling with the lid of her latte. "What are you going to do for money?"

Isn't that the million-dollar question? "I'm fine."

"Is that your way of saying you're totally fucked?"

In more ways than one. "I'm working on something, but I don't have the details figured out yet."

Her eyes spark with curiosity. "I'm going to let you off the hook—for now. Tell me what happened with Justin. You texted me that you broke up with him?"

Shame suffuses my cheeks as I remember all the times I told her how handsome he was, how perfect. "No, he broke up with me."

She looks mystified. "But he was crazy about you."

"Because of this whole mess. He said he wanted to be a senator one day, and he couldn't be connected to the James family if he was going to do that."

A gasp. "That bastard."

I look away and swallow. "I guess I understand his point. I wouldn't want to ruin his future."

"You're way too nice. He's a dirty rat bastard."

My cheeks burn as I share the most humiliating part. "I got the impression I was only going to be a stepping stone anyway. That he never really cared about me. I guess that's why he was okay waiting until marriage."

She bites her lip, looking contemplative. "I don't know about that. He was crazy about you, but he was always pretty spineless. I'm sure Papa Justin wasn't too pleased about the scandal."

I raise my eyebrows. "Spineless? You never said anything."

"I mean he looked good in a tux, but he couldn't make up his own mind about anything. He's probably following in his dad's footsteps because he couldn't think of any original career path."

I manage a wan smile. "Well, his senatorship

is safe and sound now."

"He'll regret it," she says, sounding sure. "And you're better off without him. You'll find someone who cares about you for you—not for your family name."

Maybe so, but how would that future man feel about how I'd lost my virginity? Even if I tried to keep it a secret, people would talk about it. They're paying an attendance fee just to find out my identity. After the way the reporters circled my father's court case, the entire auction might eventually be public knowledge.

I'm not just giving up my college degree or my career. I might be giving up being in love, having a family. Loneliness stretches out in front of me like a desert, Gabriel's eyes burning like the sun.

He may not be standing outside my house, but he could ask Damon what I'm doing. And he's the one who orchestrated my family's fall. He's like a puppet master, moving me faster and faster until I come apart.

"Maybe it's better that I'm not engaged. I can't focus on anything as long as Daddy's sick." He needs so much care just to stay alive. I never realized how fragile life could be until I saw all the tubes and monitors attached to his frail body. "He needs me right now."

"Don't you have a nurse for him?"

"We have someone who comes to check his medicine. The doctor comes once a week. That's all I can afford." Actually I'm running out of money for that too.

"You've been the one feeding him? Changing him?"

"When he's awake enough to eat." My stomach pitches as I remember holding in tears the last time I bathed him. It was almost worse that he was aware, feeling embarrassed that his daughter saw him naked. What choice did we have?

Compassion fills her eyes. "I would help you, but Jerk Face still controls my trust fund."

Harper was furious when her estranged father granted her stepbrother control in his will. He said it was to keep the money safe—and secretly I thought it might be for the best. Christopher is a buzzkill, but he makes sure all her bills got paid. Harper's a bleeding heart, incredibly nice but lacking practicality of any kind. She would hand over the two-thousand-dollar designer jacket off her back if a homeless person looked cold.

"In a few years I'll turn twenty-two and have control. I can help you then."

In a few years my father might be dead, but I

don't tell her that. It's not her problem. "Don't worry about us. Seriously, we're fine. It's hard right now, but it will get better."

"Because you're working on something."

Nerves churn my stomach. I'm not even sure I could back out now if I wanted to. The man outside is keeping anyone from hurting me—considering I'm worth more to Damon Scott alive than dead. What would the guard do if I tried to leave? It doesn't matter, because I can't go anywhere with my father attached to the hospital bed.

"That's right. Now tell me how long you're here. I want to stay up late and talk about what you've been doing since I left."

CHAPTER NINE

FOR TWO BLISSFUL days Harper stays with me. She told her professor that her dog at home died, which seems like a horrible lie—and not very believable either—but she has a way of wrapping men around her little finger. Except for Christopher, unfortunately.

We melt squares of butter to pour over popcorn and watch Gwyneth Paltrow in *Emma*. There aren't any other beds in the house, so we turn it into a sleepover and share my bed. She even makes her grandmother's recipe for clam chowder, which Daddy declares is delicious.

When a cab drives away with her Sunday afternoon, it feels like a cold splash of reality. The house is larger and emptier now that she's gone. After sharing the last of the chowder with Daddy for lunch, I find some clippers in the tool shed.

For the next hour I attack the wayward branches, taming the bushes along the front of the house. They don't look nearly as pretty as when we had landscapers, but that's not the point.

My hands have blistered when I finally drop the metal shears to the grass.

I head inside, intent on a shower, when I hear the phone ring.

Landon has called twice more while Harper was here, and if it's him, I'm not going to answer. The number is blocked, though, so I press the green Call button. "Hello?"

"Ms. Avery James," comes the pleased male voice. Damon Scott.

I smooth my hair back as if he can see my wild-girl appearance. I probably look like I've been hacking my way through the rain forest right now. "Oh, hi."

Paper shuffles on the line. "Are you ready for the big night?"

I'll never be ready. "Do you have a date set?"

"This Saturday. The richest men in the city are panting to find out who you are."

There's no hiding from his knowing voice on the other end of the phone, but I still duck into the pantry and shut the door. Shame burns hotly on my cheeks. *This Saturday.* "I guess that's good."

"That's excellent, trust me."

"Said the spider to the fly."

A low laugh. "This particular fly is going to get a very nice payday for her time in the web."

I hope so or this would be pointless. "I don't mean to be indelicate but…"

My breath catches because I've been taught so strenuously never to mention money. Never to appear weak. I know I need to break those habits. I'm no longer the wealthy, privileged daughter of one of the city's most venerable businessmen. But talking about money is still as hard as touching myself, forbidden for long enough to make it physically painful.

Oh God, this Saturday.

"How much money will you earn?" he says easily. "It depends on the tenor of the evening, how high we can push the bidding. I think you're looking at a couple hundred thousand, at least."

"A couple hundred…" My voice trails off, and I feel faint. At one time those kinds of numbers wouldn't have fazed me. There were savings accounts and investment funds galore. All of that has evaporated into nothing. A couple hundred thousand dollars would pay the real estate bill several times over. I'd be able to keep the house and pay for a full-time nurse.

"Maybe more. We'll have to play it by ear." I can hear his smile over the phone. "Naturally I want my percentage to be as high as possible."

"Naturally," I say, still feeling faint. I guess this is what hope feels like. "And they won't...they won't hurt me?"

I can't forget what the man said to me in the narrow hallway, about my father's enemies taking recompense out of my skin. How much can I endure for a month? Sex, definitely. But pain?

"Look, I won't lie to you," he says. "Some of the men attending dabble in some of the more...daring sexual activities, I'll say. It's a natural consequence of dealing with rich men, with too much time and money on their hands to be content with plain old vanilla."

Does he count himself in that group? Probably. I press my hand to my eyes, trying not to imagine him doing things that are daring. I especially don't want to imagine Gabriel Miller doing anything at all.

"There have to be boundaries, right?"

"Of course. You'll be the same girl coming out that you were going in. Nothing permanently harmed or changed. Except for one small portion of your anatomy."

The air in the pantry seems to get thinner. "I see."

"Don't worry. A hymen is more rare around

here than whips or chains could ever be. Hopefully you'll keep them entertained for the whole month."

"Whips and…chains?" My stomach clenches hard.

"Well, the auction begins at nine p.m. We'll start the drinks flowing before that to make sure they're loose with their wallets. You should arrive by seven to get you ready."

Two hours is a long time to get dressed. "Are you sure I need—"

"I'm sure," he says, almost cheerful. "I'll see you then."

The click over the line seals my fate.

CHAPTER TEN

IN ANCIENT MYTHOLOGY the Minotaur was a creature with the head of a bull and the body of a man. He lived at the center of a maze. Athens had to send seven young men and seven unwed girls as a sacrifice on a ship.

In my case the maze is the Den, which looms high in the dusky sky, orange rays of sunset split by the intricate turrets. There's only one sacrifice this Saturday night.

Someone waits at the curb to take my keys. I wobble on my heels for only a moment before catching myself. The last thing I need are skinned knees as I go in front of the wealthiest men in the city. Then I'm standing in the foyer, marveling as people bustle around. I hadn't quite realized how much of a production this would be, but with that much money on the line, it makes sense. My stomach pitches with nerves because I'm going to be at the center of this hurricane.

Damon emerges from a door, looking sharp in

a three-piece suit. He's one of many turns I'll take tonight, going deeper into the maze. Only at the end will I find out who's won the auction. Only then will I meet the Minotaur.

"The woman of the evening," he says warmly.

A shiver runs through me. That sounds ominous. I force myself to smile. "I'm not sure it will take me two hours to get ready, though."

He laughs. "Candy asked for the whole day. I told her she'd have to make do."

"Candy?"

"Ivan's girl. She'll be the one taking care of you."

Ivan Tabakov? I've heard his name spoken, but only in whispers. And didn't his wife used to strip at one of his clubs? I guess I couldn't ask for a better guide in the art of selling sex to dangerous men, but I'm almost more afraid of her than the men. This is a different world, requiring a different set of skills than the ones I've been building my whole life.

He directs me up the stairs and into the room where the photographs were taken.

A woman tinkers with makeup brushes on a small table against the window. I have the impression of beautiful blonde hair, long and flowing enough to make her a fairy-tale princess. Her hair might seem innocent, but her body is pure sin. The dress she wears clings to her body, accentuating her perfect curves. Good Lord. She won't be at the auction, will she? As soon as a man sees her, he won't want me. Of course, I doubt the crime boss Ivan Tabakov would be willing to share his wife.

She turns, and I'm struck breathless by her face—by the perfect heart-shaped prettiness, by the wide blue eyes. Based on the piles of makeup on the table, I had expected something over-the-top, but hers is perfectly placed to emphasize her features.

"Avery," she says, smiling. "Come in. I won't bite, I promise."

I relax by the smallest inch because she does seem genuine. In the hallowed halls I usually walk, many women will tear you down if they can get away with it. I'm so used to it that it's a shock to see someone I don't know with sympathy in her eyes. "Thank you. I'm kind of freaking out on the inside."

She reaches around me to shut the door. "We'll make those bad old men wait until you're good and ready to see them. In the meantime we'll get you cleaned up."

I flush because she makes it sound like I'm

something the cat dragged in. I can't even disagree with that assessment. Next to her I feel completely unsophisticated. "What are you going to do to me?"

Her laugh sprinkles over me like fairy dust. God, no wonder the scary mobster fell for her. "That depends on what you need, of course. Let's get that dress off and see what we're working with."

I pulled a designer evening gown out of the back of my closet, one I first wore to a senator's inaugural dinner with Justin at my side. It shows off one shoulder and has a high slit. Justin was in awe of me that night—but maybe that was manufactured, just like he pretended to care about me.

My stomach clenches for an entirely different reason than when I took my dress off in front of Gabriel. I know that she isn't looking at me like something she wants to devour, but she'll still see my insecurities. How can a woman like her understand what it's like to be too small in some places, too big in others, forever the wrong thing? How can she understand chili juice and the shame I always feel in my body?

I'm frozen with my hands clenched in fabric, my mind in a panic. How will I get through this?

She's just another turn, and I need to make it all the way to the center of the labyrinth.

Her hands grasp my shoulders and shake gently. "Avery, look at me."

After a deep breath I meet her blue gaze.

"You're beautiful, and you're brave, and you're unspeakably strong. Nothing those men do out there can change that. Got it?"

And somehow I realize she does know what it's like—the shame and the fear.

That knowledge allows me to pull the dress away and reveal myself.

She nods in satisfaction. "We'll have the boys eating out of your hand." Her gaze drops between my legs. "But first things first, that has to go."

"My panties?"

"Your hair."

I glance down, part horrified, part curious. The navy-blue panties I'm wearing cover the neatly trimmed hair underneath. "How did you—"

"How did I know? Oh honey, I've been doing this a long time." Her eyes study me as if they can read every secret that way. "You've never been completely bare, have you?"

It always felt unnecessary—and okay, a little scary. I shake my head.

She smiles, turning to a small pot that's

plugged into the wall. Something's melting inside there. *Wax.* "It's freeing, I promise. And it only hurts for a few minutes."

CHAPTER ELEVEN

AN HOUR LATER I've been waxed and primped all over my body, whimpers escaping me while she murmurs sympathetically. Now I'm wearing a robe while she does my makeup, a natural look that's somehow using more makeup than I've ever seen. Contouring, she calls it. I can't deny the effect is stunning on my cheekbones. My eyes almost look bare, even though there's shadow to make them wider. More like a doe. On my lips she paints a pale pink, like cotton candy.

"How are you feeling?" she asks.

"Relieved the waxing is over," I say honestly. I'm still feeling tender there.

"It's not my favorite part of the process, but the extra sensitivity you get will help you. And the men, they go crazy for it."

I'm not sure I've made a man go crazy for anything. "What if no one bids on me?"

She laughs softly. "Do you really think that

will happen?"

"No," I admit, but it doesn't have anything to do with confidence. I had been to enough charity auctions to know that rich old men would buy anything—broken furniture that was owned by the Queen of England, the golf ball that lost a crucial championship. "I know someone will buy me. I just don't know whether it will be enough."

There isn't an insurance policy on something like this. If someone buys me for less than the balance of that real estate bill, I'll lose the house. And I'll still have to sleep with him.

"Stand up," Candy says, her command so effortless—and so kind.

When I stand, the silk robe falls open. I gave up on modesty around the time she ripped hardened wax off my most private places, but it will be very different with a roomful of men.

She picks up a small pot of pale pink shimmer. She sweeps the brush into the powder, every move almost sensual. I'm already wearing blush, and I didn't have to stand up to apply it.

Her gaze goes to my breasts, still partially hidden by the sides of the robe.

"Oh no," I whisper.

Her expression turns sympathetic. "It might seem over-the-top, but those men are used to over-the-top. And those lights will wash you right out. This is the palest color that will work."

Her hands are gentle as they push the silk aside. The cool air brushes over my nipples, turning them into hard points. I'm shocked—in part because I wasn't sure the men would see my bare breasts during the auction. And in part because my body responds to her gaze almost with arousal.

As if I'm a work of art, she applies the brush to my nipples. She's right that it's not a drastic effect. They actually look kind of pretty like that, something I never imagined I could think.

"Men are very simple creatures," she says without looking up from my breast. "They like to feel important, to feel smart. They like to feel strong."

I wasn't sure women were so different when she put it that way. Those things sounded great to me, especially after feeling so inordinately weak. "How do you make them feel that way?"

"Not by giving in. That would be too easy."

The caress of the brush sends strange arcs of energy through my body—my chest, my sex. Even my lips seem to tingle. Every careful stroke echoes across my skin as if I'm hollow. As if there's nothing inside me but air. "So I should fight him?"

She bites her lip, concentrating. Then she stands back, examining her work. My nipple looks perfectly pink, perfectly circular. Definitely more plump than before.

One nod, then she moves to the other side. I force myself to stand still, not to demand answers, not to beg for them. "Not fight, either. I like to think of it as a dance. He steps forward, you step back. Then you step forward, and he must step back. There's a symmetry to it, a rhythm."

I blink, feeling out of my depth. "Do you mean sex?"

"That has a rhythm, but I'm talking about something more. Any woman can fuck him, any woman can spread her legs. There's nothing special with that."

"I'm a virgin." My voice comes out flat. I'm not bragging. What I so carefully protected has actually come to mean more to me than I would have expected—saving my family home. Saving my father.

I would have preferred a safe marriage. A safe life.

If I could magically change fate, I'd never want to know this desperation.

"They aren't paying for your hymen," she

says. "They're paying to teach you things. They're paying so much money because the push will be greater—but so will the pull."

The rhythm. I hear what she's saying, but I'm missing it too. She's trying to explain something to me, something important. And I know that she understands it—I know because she has a very dangerous man wrapped around her finger. I know because of the age-old wisdom in her blue eyes.

"I'm afraid," I whisper.

She gives a half smile. "That's part of the pull."

And the greater the pull, the greater the push. "The more afraid I am, the more money I'm worth?"

"It's not just fear that pulls them. Innocence and fragility and grace."

I picture the old men, smoking cigars and drinking whiskey. "Everything they're not."

Her expression turns sly. "Don't fight him, oppose him. Make him desperate for more."

I'm staring at her, wondering if she's taking her own advice—because I'm the one desperate for more. I want something concrete, some trick I can do with my hand or my tongue to make this work. Some universal safe word that will make sure I don't get hurt. Instead she's giving me philosophy.

And I'm so focused on it, so deep in it, that I don't hear footsteps in the hallway.

Don't hear the turn of the doorknob.

Then Gabriel Miller is standing in the room, his golden gaze on me. On the eyes that Candy made large and doe-like. On my pink nipples in hard little nubs. On the sensitive place between my legs, stripped bare of any covering.

The low sound he makes, almost a growl, snaps me out of the trance.

I pull the silk fabric over me, feeling exposed, abraded. I wasn't willing to examine the idea of Gabriel Miller at the auction, even though I knew he would come. He enjoys seeing me humiliated, the daughter of his enemy. It isn't enough to watch my father's fall.

He wants to see mine too.

"Damon is downstairs, holding court," he says. "Is she ready?"

Candy glances back at him, looking amused. "Of course. I was just telling her how to control whoever buys her."

His voice is bland. "Do you think he'll swing that way?"

She laughs. "Control isn't kink, darling. It's a

way of life."

The way he looks at her isn't sexual, though. There's something like respect in his eyes. Maybe it's only there because she's with Ivan Tabakov, but I don't think so. She has a way of earning it herself.

The way she leans close to me is almost regal. Her lips by my ear, she whispers, "All you have to give them is your body. Your mind, your soul— that's your leverage."

That's my ball of string, I realize. A lifeline, so I can find my way out of the maze at the end. She was playful before but dead serious at the end. Because this is life or death, my ability to move on from this. It could devastate me. It could break me.

Then she's sweeping out of the room with a little wave for Gabriel.

We're alone.

I'm insanely focused on the fact that there's only a piece of silk protecting my body from him. So thin, so vital. He doesn't stare at my body. His gaze meets mine, but I feel more vulnerable this way. He sees every doubt, every fear. "Did you touch yourself?" he asks, almost mildly.

Heat rushes to my face, and I know I'll be bright red. "That's none of your business."

He studies me, thoughtful. "I think you did, little virgin. I think you touched your hard little clit and made yourself come, your eyes squeezed shut in the dark."

I hate how well he can read me. "You don't know anything about me."

"I know I could make you come in two minutes."

A step back, my calves bumping the small chair where I sat. "You wouldn't."

"No, but you wish I would."

"I hate you."

A low laugh. "Do you really think you can control the man?"

My fists tighten in the silk, covering my breasts. "Better than the other way around."

"Would it be so bad?" he asks thoughtfully. "Giving up control for a month? Letting someone else guide you? Letting someone teach you?"

Part of me yearns for that, but not with a stranger. Not for money. "I don't care what happens to me at night. They can touch me, teach me, whatever they want. That won't really be me."

He walks to the window, looking at the city's skyline. There are people working late in those offices, climbing the corporate ladder, sleeves rolled up for the paycheck. A few of those pent-houses are empty, their occupants downstairs, waiting to bid on me.

Without turning he murmurs, "What makes you think it's only at night?"

I stare at him, unaccountably surprised. I hadn't really reasoned it out loud or I might have guessed the obvious. My knowledge of sex is so limited that I only imagine it at night. That goes doubly so for a strange old man. Uncertainty vibrates through me. "He'd want me during the day?"

Gabriel turns back, his eyes fierce. "The auction is for a month, Avery. Your days, your nights, your everything. He will own you."

A shudder squeezes my body. I'm starting to understand what Candy meant about the push. His intensity, his demands. And what would be the pull? My acquiescence. No, she told me not to give in. *Innocence and fragility and grace.*

I lift my chin, meeting his eyes. "I have to take care of my father. Someone has to feed him, to wash him. Several times a day."

Gabriel turns back to the window. "The buyer will pay for his care."

"I can't—" My voice breaks, and I suck in a steadying breath. I can't afford to pay for a full-time nurse for a month, not after paying the tax bill and Damon's percentage. What will we eat when it's over?

"He'll pay for his care," he says, his tone hard. "On top of the auction amount."

I take a step forward, strangely drawn to him. "Why would he do that?"

A large shoulder lifts. "The men down there have more money than they know what to do with. Whoever buys you, use him. Take what you need from him."

In the window I can see his reflection, the bold features of his face. But I can't read him. I could never read him. Is that part of the *push* Candy told me about? Or is that just the impenetrable mystery of Gabriel Miller? "Why are you helping me?"

"I'm not your friend," he says gently.

He's my enemy. When we're alone, it's easy to forget that. In a few minutes we'll be downstairs with the wealthiest men in the city, maybe even the state. Men who would purchase me like an object. Men who Gabriel taught a lesson by ruining my father.

"Fifteen minutes," he says before leaving the room.

CHAPTER TWELVE

FIFTEEN MINUTES FEELS like fifteen hours when you're awaiting your fate. The dress that I'm to wear is diaphanous white, almost reminiscent of ancient Greek clothing. It makes me feel more like a sacrifice for the gods—or for the Minotaur in the maze.

I'm relieved that Candy has left undergarments as well—a white bra and matching panties, made of the same satiny material as the dress. At least if someone moves the dress aside, if Damon demands that I take it off, I'll have something else to cover me.

Except if that were true, she wouldn't have bothered to paint my nipples.

I pace the room, frustrated that I can't ask her more questions, that she didn't give me more direct answers. At this point I'd even take Gabriel's company over the shameful silence.

A buzz comes from my small clutch, the one I planned to wear with my evening gown. Now I see how foolish that would have been, as if I were a guest at this party. No, I'm the main course.

The screen blinks with a new text message.

Avery, I need to talk to you.

My heart pounds. It's Justin. I haven't spoken with him since he broke up with me. There were some things I left at his apartment near campus, but none of that mattered once Daddy got hurt.

My fingers feel clumsy against the screen. *I'm busy.*

This is important, he writes. *I miss you. I made a mistake.*

Anger. Denial. Heartbreak. I felt all those things in the wake of his breakup. I have no idea how to handle this text weeks later, especially as I stand in the Den, about to be auctioned off to the highest bidder.

It's too late, I type back.

Don't say that. We can talk about this. Where are you?

Suspicion reaches for me like a cold, dark hand. *I'm out. Where are YOU?*

Your house, he says. *No one is answering the door.*

Oh my God, he's at my house. In the listless days following the breakup I would have given anything to hear that knock, to see his face. To have him say that it was a mistake.

I can't forget that Justin is a rich man, and unlike Harper, his trust fund isn't tied up with a stingy stepbrother. No, he doesn't need anyone's approval—not legally. Though most of the time he asks his dad for advice. And his dad would have told him to drop me like a hot potato.

What would have happened if Justin and I were already married when my father got convicted? What if we'd had kids already? Would Justin have stood by me then? It doesn't matter, because he didn't stand by me when it counted.

The letters blur in front of me, but I force the tears back. I won't mess up Candy's beautiful work. *I'm sorry,* I type. *It's really over.*

More than just my engagement. My life. My future?

I shove the phone back into my clutch. Did I make a mistake? My heart pounds. I imagine calling him, confessing everything, begging him to come rescue me from this tower. I can't really trust him, can't even love him, but maybe love doesn't matter in the face of cold practicality. In the face of familial duty.

And if love doesn't matter, then maybe I should accept Uncle Landon's offer. Safety, security. Isn't that worth something? God, that's worth everything.

A knock comes at the door.

My gaze darts to the whitewashed panels, wishing there was a peephole. It feels like flipping a coin—on the other side, will there be Candy's sensual advice? Or will there be Gabriel's dark threats? I know which one is safer for me, which one I should want, but as the coin rotates in the air, as I reach for the doorknob, it's Gabriel that I want to see.

Not Gabriel. And not Candy either.

It's the man from last time, the one with pale reddish hair and pale eyes. He's handsome in that stocky, filled-out way, but I can't get past the coldness of his eyes. They're light blue, but they look like ice.

He raises one tawny eyebrow, challenging me. "They're ready for you. I'm to bring you down-stairs."

And I realize what his job is tonight, guarding me. Keeping me from leaving. It's the same reason he was lurking in the hallway last time. Making sure I don't run away before I fulfill my end of the bargain. They're right to suspect me, because my doubts rise up like a black cloud.

And my father cheated Gabriel Miller. That's how I got into this mess. They would doubt my word.

You ought to be running far away. That's what he told me last time, but I know without trying now that he wouldn't let me leave. Too late to call Justin to save me. Too late to accept Uncle Landon's proposal. Fear is a cold grip on my heart.

"You're wrong," I tell him. "They won't take the money out of my skin."

They won't hurt me. I won't let them. I'll play Candy's game, like she taught me. I'll make them desperate for more, even though I'm the one who feels desperate right now.

He gives me a cruel smile. "Be glad I've got no plans to bid on you."

"What do you have against my father?"

His hand. My arm. He doesn't grip me hard, not deep enough to bruise, but I'm trapped. "He fucked over a lot of people in this town," he says. "Including me. He got his, though, didn't he? Pissing through a tube now, isn't he?"

My eyes widen. "Did you touch him?"

"I didn't hurt the fucker, but I wanted to. A lot of people did. Be careful who you trust, girl. There's plenty who want to do the same to you."

DAMON'S VOICE IS loud and booming, the perfect

auctioneer. I can hear him clearly from behind the velvet curtains. He greeted me briefly to make sure I was ready for him to introduce me. That was the word he used—*introduce.* Not sell or pimp.

Nothing dirty, even though that's what this is.

"Welcome, distinguished gentlemen—and a few lovely women. As people of discerning taste and elevated interests, I know you'll agree with me that today's auction is the event of the year. The object of our desires is waiting right now, but before I bring her out, I want to tell you a little bit about what your hard-earned money will be purchasing."

The low murmur of voices, the clink of crystal. How many people are out there?

"This particular fruit is ripe and ready to be picked," Damon continues, his tone far too pleased with himself. "I expect she'll be the perfect color when you open her up, juicy and sweet."

There's laughter in the audience, male and drunk.

"It's not only her body you'll be purchasing, though, but her mind—her ingenuity, her spark. I have here a letter of recommendation from her high school English teacher." There's a pause with a shuffle of paper. "A student of outstanding merit and exceptional integrity. And above all, a fertile mind that begs to be filled."

There's a smattering of laughter, and I flush with shame. That's not what Mrs. Stephenson wrote in my recommendation letter to college.

"Here's another one, this one from the faculty advisor for the National Honor Society." Another pause, lengthier this time. Expectation fills the air, thickening it. "Her thirst for learning is surpassed only by her desire to help others. I've never had a student with such a large…heart. And the absolute sweetest…temperament."

More laughter. I'm not sure what's more humiliating—the sexual innuendo in the fake letters? Or the fact that he's mentioning the real faculty members at my high school academy who wrote recommendation letters for me.

Damon isn't reading the actual contents, but he must have read them himself to know who they're from. My teachers were so supportive, so encouraging. And for what? So that I could stand in the center of rich men and be sold like cattle.

Of course I know who's next.

Mr. Santos was the world history teacher and the sponsor for the chess club. *Chess is a game of status and power. Of war. It's a game of human nature, Ms. James.*

I joined the chess club, not because I cared about human nature at the time, but because Daddy played with me every week. It had been the only way to win his approval, the only way to reach him.

It didn't hurt that Mr. Santos had warm brown eyes. Under his gentle tutoring I developed a major crush on him. He was nothing but proper with me, but I had the kind of teenage dreams that would have been humiliating to admit.

"And last, but certainly not least, we have the sponsor for the chess club, who says in his letter: 'Her presence at the weekly meetings was inspiring for all the other members. I'm sure the memory of her will continue to motivate the other students, who always admired her for her prodigious and impressive…talent.'"

The men respond with applause and hoots, shouting their praise for my *talents*. My stomach turns over, and I clutch my hands at my middle. I haven't eaten anything all day, which is the only reason I don't throw up all over the dark marble floors.

Daddy taught me chess.

And these men are laughing, *laughing* at it. Laughing at me.

Don't they realize that the letters are fake?

Don't they care? There are toasts to my many *large* attributes, to the sweet taste of my ambition. And I realize that it doesn't matter to them, whether the letters are true or not. It's all a big joke. My entire life, a joke.

Damon speaks over the crowd, quieting them. "Due to the *rare* nature of the object of this auction, I had to keep her identity a secret. Once you see her, I'm sure you'll understand why. And I think I've kept you waiting long enough. What do you say?"

The roar that follows makes me shrink back, away from the velvet curtain. I bump into the man with pale eyes, who stands with his arms folded, his gaze merciless. I swallow hard, almost lightheaded with panic. The small part of me that's still sane knows that Damon is whipping them into a frenzy on purpose, but that doesn't make it any less real. I'll be in the center of that thinly veiled violence.

"Come on out, darling," Damon says, his booming voice grasping hold of my throat.

I'm paralyzed. Heart, legs, eyes. Can't move a thing. Not even my lungs can draw breath. Black spots dance in front of my eyes. Am I going to pass out?

Then hands push me firmly, inexorably, from

behind. I stumble forward. The velvet curtain parts in front of me, and then I'm through the breach, standing on some kind of raised platform, looking out at a sea of faces. My mind catalogs them with chilling indifference—men in suits, ties loosened or missing, some sleeves rolled up. They sit on leather chairs strewn throughout the room, reclined, their comfort a stark contrast to my own terror.

My chest rises and falls with frantic breaths. Some of the men in the room I recognize, having met them at parties with my father, with Justin. They gave me genial smiles, seeming almost grandfatherly. They asked me about school, about my plans for the future. Now their eyes widen with shock—and something else. Vicious pleasure.

Other faces I don't recognize. They blur together.

Through the darkness I find a pair of steady golden eyes, and only then can I take a deep breath. Cool air fills my lungs, almost painful after panting in fear for so long. Gabriel leans against the back wall, all casual elegance and effortless power. I don't know whether he means to give me strength, but I take it anyway, drawing myself up straighter.

I can get through this. *I don't have a choice.*

My vision clears from the frantic blur it had been, allowing me to pick out specific faces. The sweet smell from cigars. The sharp note of whiskey. Undertones of male sweat and excitement.

Then I look at the side of the room, and everything freezes.

The whisper is torn from me, despairing. "Uncle Landon."

Chapter Thirteen

U NCLE LANDON LOOKS furious, his face contorted by accusation. He's already rising from his leather armchair, and I can't help but take a small step back. I feel like I've been caught in the act, like a parent has found me making out in the basement. But he isn't my parent at all. He tried to marry me!

He walks straight onto the platform, his features twisted into a snarl. His hand on my arm isn't anything like the man with pale eyes. I flinch at the pain, pulling away, failing.

"This was your loan? Your big plan? To become a prostitute?"

"Let go of me," I whisper because I'm not innocent in this mess—but neither is he. He would buy some virgin to use without me ever knowing. How many times would he have broken our wedding vows? They wouldn't have been born of love, but if I said *I do,* I would honor it.

"I'm getting you out of here," he says, his

voice grim. "Your father would have a heart attack if he saw you like this."

The whole room seems to cant forward, delighted with the display of fresh drama. I feel myself shrinking, as if I'm getting smaller in the middle of the room. Maybe I'll disappear into a tiny speck. And *pop* like a bubble. Surviving the auction seemed difficult, nearly impossible, but facing Uncle Landon like this breaks me completely. He's the closest person to my father, and even though I'm angry at him, I'm ashamed too.

Damon strolls closer, barely perturbed by the show of force. "You don't want to do that, Moore."

"Why not?" he demands. "She's mine. She's my fucking goddaughter."

One eyebrow lifts, mildly amused. "Then you'll want to stay and watch over her, won't you? If you continue to disrupt the auction, I'll be forced to remove you before the bidding even begins."

Uncle Landon's hands tighten on my arms, and I whimper.

Damon sighs, sounding disappointed. He doesn't seem surprised, but then he wouldn't be. Even if he didn't know that Uncle Landon was my godfather, Damon Scott knew about his close friendship with my father. "And you definitely won't get a refund on your entrance fee."

I'm trembling, caught between my future and my past. I don't really belong in either of them—I'm not cut out for this world of anger and sex, but I can never go back to my blissful naïveté either.

Gabriel appears on the platform with his large and intimidating presence. He seems to tower over all of us—Uncle Landon, me. Even Damon Scott looks smaller next to his fury.

"Release her," Gabriel says in low tones. "Unless you want your arm broken. Security here is…formidable."

Except I don't see anyone else. No bouncers or guards. Even the pale-eyed man stayed behind the velvet curtain as if he's some otherworldly creature who lurks in the dark.

There's only Gabriel, looking fierce like an avenging angel.

For a breathless moment Landon looks as if he might defy him—though I can't see how, when he would be crushed. There's more at stake than my virginity, though. Male pride. A show of strength. An example, like the one Gabriel made of my father.

This is what Candy was teaching me about.

It's what Mr. Santos taught me, too.

About war. About opposition. About standing tall in a rain of bullets.

"The show really must go on," Damon murmurs, slicing through the tension.

Uncle Landon releases me with a rough sound. "I'm glad I didn't marry you, you little slut."

My face flames with humiliation. The men circling the room couldn't hear him, but Gabriel clearly did, judging by his raised eyebrow. He doesn't wait for an explanation, though. As soon as Landon steps off the platform, Gabriel melts back into the shadows.

In minutes Damon recaptures control of the crowd's attention.

"As you can see, she's a woman of some notoriety, due to no fault of her own. An innocent woman, torn by circumstance, ruined by fate, et cetera, et cetera."

There's a smattering of laughter, and just like that, the drama is forgotten.

"We're not here to talk about what brought her to this point, though. We're here to talk about what you'll be bidding on in just a matter of minutes."

All the men stare at me, some dark gazes,

some light. One molten. All of them filled with lust, with dangerous intent. They want to fuck me. Do they want to hurt me? And if they do, is it because they're bored with vanilla, as Damon seems to think? Or because they want revenge against my father?

There are a few women in the audience. Would the women bid on me, or are they just arm candy?

On the opposite side of Landon, I see Ivan Tabakov in a large wingback chair. Candy is perched on his lap, her heels tipped over at his feet, her toes curled up on his leg. She looks like a child with large blue eyes and fairy-tale hair.

Another woman looks even younger than me, her dress revealing more than it hides. She hangs on the arm of a gray-haired man like I imagine she would at some high-rollers casino, both glamorous and mercenary.

The other woman appears older, beautiful but hard. Almost cruel. She sits at one of the only small leather love seats with another man. Their sides touch intimately—husband and wife? Both of their gazes examine my body with mean promise.

It wouldn't only be the husband who hurt me; that much I know.

"One full month," Damon says, circling behind me. "That's how long you would have to train this lovely specimen in the erotic arts. Such thirsty...intellect, they said. What would you do with her?"

"Play chess," Gabriel says from the back of the room, his voice droll.

The men in the room laugh, and I feel my stomach turn over.

Apparently this is the cue Damon needs to stop pretending it's my intellect they're interested in. He begins describing my physical characteristics with a bluntness that steals my breath.

"Her skin is pale milky perfection, her hair's a mix of gold and copper. She also has very large...eyes, as you can see. And she narrows most delectably...on the bridge of her nose. Then flares again...on her wide mouth."

He isn't talking about my face. He's talking about my body. My hands are clenched at my sides, my entire body strumming with the urge to flee. I can't forget the rouge on my nipples. Everyone will see them before this auction ends.

"Take it off," one of the men yells, his voice slurred.

"Do you want to see more?" Damon asks, his tone solicitous, as if this is a polite affair. Instead it feels like a bullfight. I'm the animal, made to run and run while my body bleeds.

"Yes," they shout, stomping their feet. It feels like a riot. "Take it off!"

Damon doesn't look worried, though, merely pleased. He touches the small hidden clasp on my shoulder and the top of the dress falls away, revealing the downy slopes of my breasts, the white lace of the bra.

"Almost there," he murmurs.

Another flick of his fingers at my back, and the bra slides forward. He nudges gently, moving the straps down my arms, tickling my skin with lace, making me prick with shame. My arms cling to the material until it hangs nearly at my wrists.

Painfully, almost against my will, I unclench my fists. The bra falls to the floor.

My pink nipples tighten in the exposed air, and the crowd roars their approval.

"They would fill a man's hands, don't you think?" he calls over the crowd.

There's more shouting, more salacious specu-lation about the rest of me. What color would my pussy lips be? How tight is my cunt? I stand very still, unable to glance at Uncle Landon—to see the condemnation in his eyes. Or worse, the lust. I can't even look for Gabriel. Is he shouting with the rest of the men? Is his voice demanding that I be passed around for inspection? I can't bear to know, so I stare straight ahead, the yellow glow of the lamps blurring as my eyes sheen with tears. A deep breath. I won't cry in front of them. They paid for my body, not for my despair.

"Let's start the bidding at twenty thousand," Damon says, and almost every placard rises in the air. The sea of red paddles, each with a black engraved number, makes my stomach churn.

Damon turns into a master auctioneer, speaking faster and faster.

"Can I get twenty-five, twenty-five? I have twenty-five. Thirty! What about thirty-five? You'll have this girl for thirty days and thirty nights, yours to do as you please, surely that's worth— thirty-five! Do I have forty-five?"

My gaze darts around the room, trying to keep up with the bids. The number goes higher and higher, and as if we're climbing a mountain, the atmosphere seems to thin. I have to breathe twice as fast to get enough oxygen.

Fifty thousand dollars. What will they expect me to do for that much money? What will I have to endure? I almost wish it had stopped lower.

I look at Candy, who has her hands curled up like a child, her head tucked under Ivan Tabakov's chin. He looks hard and foreboding above her, like he's carved out of stone—but I know from her contentedness that she's completely safe in his arms. I'm longing for that security, standing on a pedestal, my pride ripped to shreds.

"Fifty," Damon says sadly. "That's all for this ripe peach?"

He grasps the fabric at my hips and pulls, leaving my legs bare. I'm only wearing the plain white panties in a roomful of people. I can't help it—I cover myself, my hands cupping between my legs. This seems to delight Damon, who laughs. The rest of the room stomps their approval, raising their glasses and toasting one another.

Beautiful find, one of them says, like I'm an archeological dig.

Perfect rack. Look at those hips. I'm too busy looking at her mouth. I'd keep those lips busy, that's for fucking sure. More laughter.

My gaze snaps to Gabriel Miller. He leans against the back of the wall, arms crossed. He isn't even holding a placard, but that doesn't surprise me. He's here to see me humiliated, not because he wants me. No, the surprising part is the faint whisper of disappointment. I should know better than that, because if anyone would take my father's debt out of my skin, it would be him.

"Imagine tasting her," Damon says. "Imagine pressing her sweet flesh between your fingertips."

There are a few men in the audience who haven't raised their placards yet.

Maybe they don't like what they see—my body or my family name. Or maybe they only paid the entrance fee to watch the spectacle. But now they lean forward and begin bidding. I realize that they were waiting for the preliminary bids to get out of the way.

These are the serious bidders.

They mean to win.

"Do I have seventy-five, seventy-five, seventy-five?"

Uncle Landon raises his placard, his eyes coldly trained on me.

A gasp escapes me. "No," I whisper. Not when I turned down his marriage proposal and the security that would have come with it. Not when he reminds me of my father.

Not when he really wants my mother.

Part of me hopes that he's bidding to save me. Maybe he'll send me home without making me fulfill my end of the bargain. But his gaze rakes my body, leaving no doubt about his plans. And part of me burns in anger because my father considered him a friend—and when my father most needed help, Uncle Landon turned his back.

Oh, he helped me spend the last of the money. He explained the limitations of my trust. But if he could spend seventy-five thousand dollars on my virginity, he could have saved our house himself.

The man with the beautiful blonde on his arm outbids him. If I were to guess, I'd say he purchased her as well. Probably the terms were more subtle than an auction. Gifts. An allowance. The principle is the same. Why does he need another woman? How many does he own?

Uncle Landon outbids him, leaning forward in his seat.

Eighty thousand. Ninety.

One hundred twenty.

One hundred twenty-five.

My stomach clenches and unclenches in rapid succession, and I'm afraid I'm going to hurl even without having eaten. Maybe I'll just make horrible, unsexy sounds as I heave, causing everyone to give up on the auction and go home.

Damon drives the bidding higher. The gray-haired man and Uncle Landon continue to fight each other, pushing the number up, locked in a stalemate like bucks fighting with their horns.

One hundred eighty-five. One hundred ninety.

Two hundred thousand dollars. Uncle Landon's placard stares back at me, unmoved by my horror. I want to pretend that I misunderstood the bidding, but Landon's expression of gruesome triumph proves he won. I'm going home with him to spread my legs, to pretend to be my *mother.*

Everyone in the room turns to look at the gray-haired man. Even the beautiful woman on his arm seems tense with anticipation, waiting to see if he'll continue to bid.

"Do I have two hundred thousand and ten?" Damon says almost casually.

The gray-haired man studies my body with a clinical expression. He narrows on the space between my legs, the patch of white fabric. "Let's see her."

Immediately the crowd erupts into expressions of agreement, demands to remove my panties.

Damon seems to consider this request. "You have to pay to play, my friend."

The gray-haired man gives a European shrug. "It won't break her virginity just to look."

A long pause where my legs press together, knees weak. Oh God, I can't do this. Can't pretend to be my mother, can't bare everything for strangers. I can't wake up, and the nightmare's only just begun.

Damon turns to me in the silence. The entire room seems to hold its breath.

I meet Damon's eyes and see a glimmer of sympathy. No no no. He'll make me undress for them. And what next? Would they get to inspect me?

To feel between my legs and verify that my hymen is still intact?

Tears burn my eyes, and I know I won't be able to hold them back. I pray for strength and find none. That feels like losing more than anything else—more than being naked, more than being sold.

Letting them see how much it hurts.

"One million dollars."

The room goes deathly silent. It might have all been a dream, and when I open my eyes, I'll still be pacing the room upstairs, waiting to be called down. I can't hear a single dirty suggestion, the clink of ice in a glass.

When I look up, Gabriel stands in front of the platform. Even with an extra foot of platform underneath my feet, he's taller than me. I look up at him, searching his eyes for some hint of kindness, of mercy. There's none. I find only fire—

and the thought that comes next makes me shudder: this is vengeance. It's not a feeling he's had, a fleeting thought for revenge. This is what he's made of, cell by cell, atom by atom. He's pure fury, and he's coming for me.

"Well," Damon says, sounding quite pleased. Chuffed, that's how I'd describe him.

Gabriel takes a step onto the platform, and I take a step back.

"Why?" I whisper urgently. I need to know what he wants with me. They're not just buying my virginity. Even Candy told me that. And it's doubly true with a man as complex, a man as fierce as him.

A slight shake of his head is his only answer.

Damon watches us with a benevolent half smile. "Ladies and gentlemen, I believe we have our winner. Unless anyone would like to—"

Gabriel makes that growling sound again, and Damon laughs softly. "Sold for one million dollars!"

CHAPTER FOURTEEN

IN THE MYTH of the Minotaur, Theseus, son of King Aegeus, decides that he will slay the monster. He runs the beast through with a sword and then retraces his steps using the string, thus saving all the sacrifices that year and in the future.

I've reached the center of the maze.

I'm facing my very own Minotaur. His eyes glow with fierce possession. His hand captures mine, and then he's pulling me down from the platform. We walk quickly through the haphazard leather chairs. He ignores the shouts and catcalls to share me. I still don't have my shift or a bra. I'm naked down to my panties, and the last glimpse they have of me is my backside covered in white. Then we're alone in a room with dim lamps and a fire in the hearth. Even with the heat, I shiver. Gabriel pulls off his jacket and wraps it around my shoulders.

Candy couldn't give me a sword, but maybe she left me a ball of string. Hope to find my way back to myself when all of this is over. Maybe someday I'll return to college. I'll find love with a regular man and lead a normal life. I have to believe that, because if I have to wander these halls the rest of my life, I'll go insane.

"Why did you bid on me?" My voice shakes.

Gabriel crosses the room and pours himself a glass of something amber. He takes a deep swallow. "For the same reason the other men did."

The small hope that I hadn't even wanted to acknowledge, the wish that someone would save me, dies in that moment. "Of course you did."

He returns and hands me the glass. I take a sip and cough as it burns down my throat. Then I take another sip. Immediately I feel fortified, and I realize I should have started with this. In only a few pulls the world seems a little warmer, the sharp edges softened. I hand back the glass and pull the lapels of his jacket closed in front of me, hiding my extra-pink nipples.

"My stuff is upstairs," I whisper, my gaze darting anywhere but at him. Will he take me to that little room and fuck me there? Or will he do it in this room on an old leather armchair?

He gives a rough laugh. One last swallow and the glass is empty. "Already making demands, little virgin?"

I blink because I hadn't thought I could demand anything. Hadn't believed I'd have power. I'm already nothing, but inch by inch he reminds me that I'm even less. "It's just…" My voice breaks. "My purse. My phone. A dress."

Because I'm naked under his jacket, which barely covers the place between my legs. I can feel cool air from the room slip underneath my panties with no hair to protect me. Everything feels more exposed down there, more vulnerable since Candy pulled the wax away.

And then there are my breasts.

The silk lining his jacket rubs against me. Candy was right about the lights washing me out in that dark room, spotlights aimed at the platform, but here in this room with just him and me, the rouge on my nipples highlights what he's going to do to me.

He takes a step toward me, and I back up. Another step. Another. My back hits the wall, and I turn away from him. He grips my chin and makes me face him. His gaze burns with lust, with possession. With an intensity that whips straight to my core.

"Let's get one thing straight," he says, his breath gentle against my forehead. "I bought you.

You're mine. You go where I say, when I say. And you do whatever the fuck I tell you to do."

I manage not to flinch. *A million dollars.*

Meeting his gaze, I let him see the core of strength inside me, however thin, however deep. He can touch my body, but he can't touch that. I told him as much upstairs. "Got it."

"Yes, sir," he says.

My stomach clenches in instinctive refusal. I press my lips together, facing him with mutiny in my expression. *Would it be so bad?* he asked me. *Giving up control for a month? Letting someone else guide you? Letting someone teach you?* Reluctantly I mutter, "Yes, sir."

The corner of his lips turns up. "Don't fight me, little virgin. I'll enjoy it too much."

That's probably true. I lift my chin, determined to face whatever he throws at me. "What should I do?" I ask, challenging. "Should I get on my back? Or on my hands and knees?"

"Still trying to control things," he muses.

I look away. "No, I'm trying to give you what you paid for."

"That might have worked with one of those assholes in there."

He reaches up to toy with a strand of my hair, almost tender. Then thick fingers push through the dark blonde locks. His fist clenches. I make a keening sound as he yanks my head back, his golden gaze looking down at me. My lips are parted in shock and pain—and something too dark to name.

He studies my face, almost in reverence. "Here's the thing about owning a virgin. For as long as I don't fuck you, I still own one."

My breath catches. Does that mean he's giving me a reprieve? Or does he have darker things in mind for me? He doesn't have to fuck me to hurt me. He doesn't have to take my virginity to get revenge.

"Are you going to hurt me?"

A soft breath of amusement. "Did Candy tell you all about her kinky games?"

I feel my eyes widen. She likes kinky games? I remember her tucked into Ivan's lap like a child, legs pulled up underneath her, hands folded almost in prayer. "She told me not to give in."

His smile spreads, slow and unbearably sexy. A man like him has no right to look that handsome. He should look like his insides: dark and cruel. "Good," he says simply. "It will be more fun."

She told me other things, that by opposing him I would make him desperate for more. I don't share that with Gabriel. He wouldn't be afraid. He'd like the challenge of it.

He pushes back from me, his lids lowered. "We're leaving."

My hands tighten on his jacket. Every time I squeeze the fabric, a faint burst of masculine spice fills the air. "I have to go home, at least. I'm not trying to control you, but my dad—"

"He's taken care of."

I suck in a breath because that sounds more like a threat than reassurance. "What does that mean?"

"A nurse is already with him. Tomorrow morning she'll be replaced with the day nurse."

How did he manage that so quickly? Except that's what money can do. It was only a year ago that I had money, my father's money, but I've almost forgotten how powerful it can be.

"How do I know you're telling the truth?"

"Christ." He cups his hand around my neck, his fingers tightening enough to make me gasp. "Do you know what I would do to a man who questioned my word?"

Don't give in. I meet his gaze even though my eyes are watering, my lungs are burning. "Then do it," I whisper. "If you don't want to fuck me, then fucking do it."

He looks at me like I'm some kind of other-worldy species. Then he grins, for a fleeting second seeming unaccountably younger. His hand falls away, and I blow out a breath. "You'll have to trust me, little virgin. If I wanted your father dead, he would be."

A shiver runs through me. The words shouldn't be reassuring, but somehow they are. For Gabriel Miller the most important thing is his word, which is why my father's cheating had to be punished. Which means that I can trust him...up to a point.

He won't lie to me, but he would honestly hurt me.

A buzz comes from the table with the drinks, and he crosses the room to his phone. A quick glance at the screen. "My car is outside."

I look down at my bare legs. The jacket is large enough to cross over my front, but one wrong step, one gust of wind, and they'll see everything. "But…"

His expression turns dark. He reaches for me, and I flinch. Eyes of burnished gold narrow. When he grasps me behind my neck, I can't help the low sound of animal fear that escapes me. With only that touch on my body, he leads me out of the room and into the hallway. Distantly I hear the sound of raucous laughter, of feminine moans. Did Damon bring out more women for them, nonvirgin consolation prizes?

Holy shit. A million dollars.

We head the other direction, toward the front door. I cringe as the door opens, revealing slick pavement and a driver standing beside a limo. By luck or by design, there's no one else on the street.

I take one step over the threshold and then shriek as my entire body is lifted into the air. My bare feet never touch the wet concrete. I'm sideways in Gabriel's arms, the jacket askew, hopelessly revealed for anyone to see. I only catch a glimpse of the valet averting his eyes before I'm tossed unceremoniously onto the leather seats. Gabriel steps inside after me. The limo glides forward.

CHAPTER FIFTEEN

AS ARMOR GOES, the suit jacket leaves a lot to be desired. It has beautiful stitching, expensive fabrics, but it's tailored to fit a man much larger than me. And it has the musky scent of him, a constant reminder that we're both possessions. Soon I'll smell like him too.

He deposits me in a room as easily as he might sling his jacket over the chair. It's a strange room but a comfortable one. A deep-set wraparound couch fills most of the space, the pillows covered with canvas that has sketches of random objects—an antique typewriter, an old-looking telescope. One wall has exposed brick, not the industrial red brick of Justin's loft, but a beige and brown mosaic that feels almost soft. A large burnished iron chandelier casts yellow light on the dark wooden beams that crisscross the white ceiling.

On a small end table there's a shiny silver phone with a circle for numbers. I wonder if it's functional. And if it is, I should probably call home and make sure a nurse is actually with my father.

Then again, I already did our evening routine before I left for the auction. I might use the time better by taking a drink from the bar setup with a copper rolling cart. How hard will this be? How much will it hurt? Judging by the way he cornered my body against the wall in the Den, estimating the size of his body relative to mine, quite a lot. Something amber-colored or even clear ought to fortify me.

Then the door opens, and Gabriel stalks inside. He reclines on the corner of the large sectional, one leg slung over the other, his shirt-sleeves rolled up, revealing deeply tanned forearms. He isn't a man who gives orders from the comfort of an air-conditioned penthouse office.

"Getting comfortable?" he asks, his expression unreadable.

"Should I be?"

"You'll be here for a month," he says, which doesn't really answer the question.

"In this room?" I ask, keeping my tone bland. Like his. "In this suit jacket? Or will there be a bed and clothes at some point?"

"God, your tongue," he says with a groan that reverberates through my body. "We're going to have so much fun, your tongue and I."

That sounds ominous, but of course it does. Everything he says is designed to scare me. Everything he does is designed to knock me down. That's part of the push and pull that Candy warned me about, but that doesn't make it any less real. That doesn't make it any less terrifying. How did she remain so calm in the face of this? How was her expression so serene curled up in the arms of a killer? She's a puzzle I haven't figured out, and it feels somehow imperative that I do.

"Look at you," he murmurs. "You know just enough to be scared, don't you?"

I shake my head because I don't know anything. I've heard about blowjobs and sex. Harper's even told me about anal sex, how two men can have you at the same time. It's not his sex that scares me—it's power. What will Gabriel Miller do to me tonight? Will he rip away the jacket and throw me to the floor? Will he thrust inside me, fast and hard and merciless?

He looks considering. "I could tell you there's pleasure too, but that wouldn't help you, would it?"

"That scares me too," I whisper. It actually scares me worse, because pain would be easy to hate. Pleasure is a strange concept to a girl who's lost everything, far too tempting.

He nods, gesturing to the floor at his feet. "We won't start there. Not for you. Kneel, little virgin. There's something you need to learn."

I almost don't make it across the two feet of deep shaggy rug. My knees buckle when I'm in front of him, folding my body like an accordion. Then I'm shivering in front of him, wrapped up in Italian fabric, a package waiting to be torn open.

His touch is achingly gentle—a single finger, the blunt of it on my collarbone. Only that, and my skin tightens beneath his touch. Fighting him? Welcoming him? I don't know, but when he trails his finger lower, pushing the suit lapel aside, I go cold. My hands unclench in degrees, allowing him to pull the suit jacket open.

He leans forward, elbows on his knees, gaze meeting mine. "Did he see these?"

My nipples tighten as I remember the hungry gaze of every man in that room. "Everyone saw them."

"I mean that fucker who put a ring on your finger."

Justin, who at this moment might be at my father's house. "He saw them."

"Did he touch them? Lick them? Put clips on your nipples?"

Deep inside I feel something twist, the turning of a screw. "No."

"Pretty little virgin," he says, almost sad.

There's something feral about this man, a fire that burns inside him, untamed. He could have tossed me down as soon as we got in the house. He could have fucked me on that platform for an audience if he wanted to. As hard as this is, it could have been worse.

Gabriel didn't buy my hymen, that's what Candy said. He bought the right to teach me. And in the same way, I didn't sell my virginity. I bought security. An unlikely tenderness surges within me. I place a hand on his thigh, intimidated by the warmth of him through his slacks, the hardness of the muscles I feel. But I won't be deterred. Not when I know the gray-haired man wouldn't have been so patient.

"You can touch them," I say, feeling almost shy. "You can...lick them. If you want."

He looks at me, almost disbelieving. "Christ."

"Or should I do it to you?"

"A blowjob?"

I assume that's coming, especially if he wants to continue to own a virgin, as he put it. "I can lick your nipples." Embarrassment heats my cheeks. "Does that feel good for you?"

He's completely still a moment, a statue made of stone.

Then he leans forward, grasps my hair in his fist, and shakes. "You're so fucking innocent. Do you get that? So fucking breakable."

He seems almost angry, but I don't understand. I thought he liked my innocence. I thought that was the whole point. In the face of his fury, my lack of knowledge feels shameful. I shrink back, but his grip holds me tight. "What did I do wrong?" I ask, my voice even.

"Nothing," he says, almost a snarl. "You're fucking perfect. An angel. A sacrifice on a marble altar. You'll give up every part of yourself just to save your precious fucking father, won't you?"

He pushes me aside and strides from the room, slamming the door behind him.

I suck in deep breaths where I've fallen on the plush rug. Shock and fear form a toxic mixture inside me. I held out hope that my father's complete and total ruin would be enough for Gabriel Miller. Held out hope he wouldn't want to take it out on me. Now I realize how innocent that hope was. The pale-eyed man was right—the debt would be taken out of my skin.

And the fact that he hadn't fucked me quickly isn't a kindness. It means that he'll make it slow. That he'll draw out my torture. That he will make every penny count.

CHAPTER SIXTEEN

W HEN I CATCH my breath, I don't waste my
opportunity. I stand on wavery legs and
head straight for the copper liquor cart. There are
a large assortment of bottles and decanters, some
of them with labels. Jack Daniels and Anejo
Tequila.

The only alcohol I ever tasted is a few stolen
sips of champagne at a society party. I can't know
that these bottles are expensive, except the rest of
the house is expensive. And I suspect that a few of
the bottles are made of actual gold and platinum,
not just colored metal. There's a crown of small
diamonds on one of them. God, does he just
throw this away when he's drunk it all? The excess
of the wealthy bothered me sometimes, but it
seems almost cruel now that I'm broke.

Excess or not, I'm not going to drink his super
expensive alcohol. For all I know he'd bill me for
every thousand-dollar sip. He isn't actually that
petty, especially with the casual way he accepted

the responsibility of a nurse for my father without argument. But I still would feel too strange even touching those bottles, like a small child playing with her mother's jewelry.

Near the back of the cart, tucked behind some wine, I spot a plain-looking bottle of clear liquid. There's a label, but it's scrawled by hand, the blue ink faded. I squint and try to make out the words. The date's about ten years ago—probably the newest alcohol on this cart. And definitely the cheapest. It's almost full. He wouldn't notice if I took a small shot. He wouldn't care.

At least that's what I tell myself when I rummage through the glasses for the smallest one. It's small and square-shaped with a thick, heavy bottom. I twist open the top and pour a splash in. So small.

"Here's to nothing," I murmur before throwing back the shot the way I've seen in movies.

The liquid burns down my throat and then throughout my body, spreading like a flame, and I cough, struggling to breathe. Dear God, that tastes like rubbing alcohol. If rubbing alcohol were on fire. That can't be how alcohol is supposed to taste, can it? No wonder he had this one shoved to the back.

I can't deny that as the burn fades I feel a little

more relaxed. I suppose that means it's doing its job. If this is what alcohol does to people, no wonder they drink.

Liquid courage. That's what it's called, and I use the courage to pick up the silver phone. Look at that, the rotary circle actually turns. I don't know the number to the night nurse who's supposedly there. And our landline was one of the first expenses to go when things turned bad.

Instead I dial Justin, because he's where I need him to be. It's almost sweet, if he hadn't turned his back on me when I needed him most.

"Hello?" His voice sounds the same. We might be meeting up for coffee on one of his visits in town. He might be greeting someone at a party while I smile from beside him.

A pang of regret hits my chest. "It's me."

"There you are. God, Avery, I've been calling you. What the hell is going on?"

I take another drink and find it doesn't burn quite as hot this time. The pain is almost pleasant. "Are you still at my house? Did a nurse show up there?"

"Yeah, about the same time as I got here. She was dressed in scrubs or something, and she had a key, but she said I had to wait outside in my car."

At least Gabriel was telling the truth about

getting a nurse for my father. In fact if that timing is correct, the nurse actually showed up before the auction finished. Maybe that was Damon's doing, preparing for what would surely follow. He wouldn't have wanted anything to interfere with his percentage.

"I'm going to be gone for a little while. A month."

"A month? What are you talking about, Avery? And where the hell are you?"

The exasperation in his voice makes me wince. At one time I would have bent backward to placate him, to reassure him that his needs came first. Now I take another drink. "It's kind of a long story."

"You sound funny. Are you... You aren't drinking, are you?"

"It's so good, Justin," I whisper as if I'm letting him in on a secret. "So bad but so good."

He swears, using words I've never heard him use. "Are you at an event?"

The museum donor event. A charity dinner that costs a thousand dollars a plate. That's what he means, and I can't help the giggle that bubbles up. It doesn't even feel awful anymore, just kind of funny. "Everyone stopped talking to me around the time you did. We don't get invited anymore, and even if we did, we couldn't afford to go."

I have this random picture in my head of pushing my dad's hospital bed like it's a wheelchair, smiling at everyone while we eat our fast-food burgers stashed in my purse. Whatever's in this bottle tastes like battery acid, but it feels *amazing*.

"Avery, listen to me," he says in this exasperated voice that means he's had to repeat himself. Just for that I take another drink. "Tell me where you are and I'll come get you."

Would he really? I don't even know where the limo drove us, but if he found Gabriel Miller's address, would he come riding up on a white steed? I don't know if I believe that he wanted to get back together, or that he still would once he sees inside my house. All those empty rooms. We could have one of those flash raves where they fill the room with soap suds and save on cleaning.

"Justin," I say in what I hope is my serious voice. I make the *n* sound last a long time to be sure. "Would you have bid on me? Do you even have a million dollars?"

"What are you talking about?" he says, his voice getting louder.

As if I can't hear him, which I totally can. I

take another gulp, larger this time. That's my new drinking game—a drink whenever he gets mad. If I'd done this at our last few appearances, I would have had a *much* better time.

And why did I never notice that he called our dates appearances?

"I'm talking about social climbing," I say, examining the bottom of the cup. All gone. "You are a social climber. And I am a social faller."

Then I collapse into a fit of giggles. Somehow the silver phone handle ends up dangling off the end table, Justin's voice a cartoonish buzz. I picture him as a tiny little man on my shoulder, like when an angel and a devil appear to whisper advice in your ear. Would he be the angel? Candy would definitely be the devil.

The chandelier is so big. It must weigh like eight tons. I realize I'm lying on the floor, looking up at it. What if it fell on me right now? Game over. That's what would happen. No maze, no sword. No sailing back with a white flag on my ship.

That was the agreement Theseus made with his father. If he was successful in killing the Minotaur, he would wave a white flag from his ship on return. Except in all the excitement he forgot. His father watched the ship approach with so much grief he killed himself.

That's always been the saddest part of the story. It was all for nothing. *I'll wave the white flag, Daddy.* And I'd never let him know what I did to save the house. I didn't want him to die.

"Christ," a voice says, low and rumbly. Not at all like the tiny angel Justin.

Gabriel's face fills the space above my head, blocking the millions of lights from the chandelier.

"Oh, hi."

He looks incredulous. "You're drunk."

"I can't be drunk. I only had one glass. And don't worry, I drank the cheap stuff."

The empty glass must have rolled under the rug. He picks it up and sniffs. "You drank moonshine?" He makes a low growling sound. "This was the last bottle my dad made before he died."

My mouth drops open. "Oh my God, the white flag."

His gaze narrows on the phone. "Who did you call?" He doesn't wait for me to answer but strides over to pick up the hanging shiny handset. "Who is this?"

"Don't you like caller ID?" I ask curiously. The silver rotary phone is pretty, but it doesn't seem practical. Then again he just paid one million dollars to have sex with me. Maybe practicality isn't a priority for him.

He slams the phone down, vibrating with some kind of intense emotion. "Who. Did. You. Call?"

I grew up around important men. Powerful men. Angry men. I learned to speak softly, to tread lightly. To smile at them and touch their arm, as if everything I do is to placate them. It's not because I think they're better than me. It just makes life easier. Then I disappear into my books, into the myths that make up a fantastical world so far removed from my own.

Except somehow I've stepped into that world—a place of gods and monsters. My diplomacy might serve me well now, except the moonshine seems to have stripped it all away.

"I called my fiancé, Mr. Nosy Pants."

His eyes darken. "He isn't your fiancé anymore."

"He said he wants to get back together."

Gabriel comes to stand directly over me, his gaze intense. "That's not happening. I bought you. You're fucking mine. Got it?"

I giggle. "He's going to be so mad once he finds out. Men are always so mad."

"He can fucking deal with me if he has a

problem with it."

My fingers form a frame in front of me, and I look at him between them. "You're handsome for a monster."

"Thank you," he says through gritted teeth. "Do you want to get up off the floor now?"

I manage to sit up, but then the world spins. "I'm thirsty. I need more of that moonshine."

"No."

"Are you saving it?" I whisper. "Since it's the last moonshine your daddy made?"

"I was," he says, his voice dry.

I nod. "I can drink the Crown Royal instead. Or the tequila. I've never had tequila."

"No more drinks for you. It's bedtime."

"What? That's *so* unfair." I haven't had a bedtime since I graduated from high school. And even though I usually went to bed by curfew at college, he doesn't have to know that. "I'm not even sleepy."

As the words leave my lips, a wave of tiredness washes over me. It feels like more than the normal amount of sleep that you feel at the end of the night. This feels like I've been walking through the desert for days. It weighs down my eyelids until I'm looking at Gabriel through half-mast.

He shakes his head. "Do not throw up on

me."

I don't know what he means until his hands slide under my legs. Then behind my shoulders. And I'm in the air, held only by his strength. I curl myself against his linen shirt, breathing in the musky scent of him. "You smell good."

"You smell like a distillery."

He's taking me somewhere upstairs, and I close my eyes. "It will hurt less like this."

"It won't hurt at all," he says, softer now. "I'm putting you to bed."

"Because you want to own a virgin," I say, repeating him.

He doesn't answer, nudging a door open. I glance around to see heavy brocade curtains and a high bed in the middle of the room. Lavender flowers adorn the thick down comforter, setting off the pale yellow vertical stripes on the wall. Pretty.

"Too pretty for you," I murmured.

"You're probably right about that," he says, sounding amused.

"I'm going to kill you."

"Is that right?" he says, sounding less amused.

"With a sword."

"And where are you going to get a sword?" He lays me down on sheets that feel outrageously cool against my heated skin. Then he pulls up the blanket. I think it's going to be too hot, but once they're on top of me, they feel just right.

"I haven't figured that out," I say with a sigh. It's a puzzle, that's for sure. "But I don't want to kill you. I just don't want to die."

He's silent a moment, and I peek one eye open at him. He's looking at me with a strange expression. I would almost describe it as tender if he didn't have the head of a bull.

"Give me the jacket," he says gently.

Only then do I remember the jacket that's wrapped around me. It has been ever since the auction. I guess it's his way of claiming me, of marking me. So why does he want it back? I know he won the auction, but the jacket feels like my trophy.

"Do I have to?"

"You'll be more comfortable."

"Everything feels so good. You should have some of that moonshine."

"I'll think about it," he says roughly. "The jacket?"

"Don't look," I warn him.

After a moment he turns and faces the door. Only then do I shrug out of the big suit jacket. God, his shoulders must be massive to fit this.

And his biceps. God. I can see them through his shirt, bulging. It looks obscene. Like if there was a Playboy magazine spread open on the bed, his muscled forearms would be more explicit.

I put the jacket on top of the bedspread and snuggle back under the blanket, all the way up to my neck. This is the softest bed I've ever lain in. "Ready."

He turns around and picks up the jacket. Then he stands there looking at the fabric in his hands as if he can't quite figure something out. As if he can't quite figure *me* out, even though I'm so simple. Simple girl, simple dreams. College, marriage, kids. A family—a real family, not just a dad who works through dinner most days. He's the mystery.

I glance at the other side of the bed. "Are you going to sleep…you know? Over there?"

He looks at the empty space on the bed, his expression brooding. "No."

That makes sense, because this can't be his room. It's way too pretty. Way too feminine. He probably sleeps somewhere with glass and sleek black lines. With a TV set into the wall and real fur on the bed. Maybe there are animal horns nailed to the wall.

"Avery," he says, still holding the jacket like

it's something precious.

I blink as sleep overtakes me. "Yes?"

"Be careful. I'm more dangerous than you know."

The slightest awareness creeps back into me, along with a cold feeling. I shiver beneath the down blanket. I can sense how dangerous he is, but the knowledge doesn't help me. I'm trapped here. I'm his. "Did you hurt my dad?"

"He deserved everything I did to him."

My fists clench beneath the covers. "Why are you telling me this?"

"Because I don't want you to die either."

He looks at me for another moment before turning to leave. The lights go dark, and my mind blurs. I know this is important, that he told me something important, but the moonshine turned my brain to mush. Sleep is inky and dark, thick as it swallows me whole.

Be careful, he said, but even as I drift away, I can't remember why.

Chapter Seventeen

THE NEXT MORNING I wake up with a headache from hell. On shaking legs I stumble across the plush carpet, wearing only a white lace thong to prove anything happened last night. I don't have any energy for modesty, though, and the room is empty anyway. Oh thank God, there's a brand-new toothbrush on the counter. After I've brushed my teeth and washed my face, I feel maybe ten percent more human. Enough that I can peek back into the room. Still empty.

A patch of white on the dresser catches my eye. I find a note scrawled with the phone number for the place handling my father's nurses. I recognize the name of one of the high-end private agencies from when I called around.

I wasn't able to afford them.

On the chair beside the dresser sits my purse. I dig inside and find my phone. First things first, I dial the number. As soon as I tell them my name, they transfer me immediately to a Mr. Stewart, the director of the facility. I never got past the front-desk girl before.

"We have our absolute best nurses working with him," he assures me. "Over thirty years of experience between them, excellent references. The utmost discretion, of course."

"Thank you," I say, my voice faint.

"They're in direct communication with his doctor—we got your consent form, of course. To make sure he remains comfortable during your brief sojourn."

Sojourn? That's a new way of describing prostitution.

Mr. Stewart gives me his personal phone number and implores me to call him anytime, day or night, if I want to check on my father. It's an outrageous level of service, even for the price that I was quoted. I'm sure Gabriel is paying more than that for this kind of attention. Or maybe it's his name on the check that demands such respect.

An uneasy feeling twists my stomach. I should feel good that my father is taken care of. Certainly these nurses will be able to provide better care than I could. But I can't help feeling that I'm somehow in Gabriel Miller's debt. And as my father learned, that's a terrifying place to be.

I find most of my clothes in the closet, hanging neatly. God, how hard had I been sleeping? That moonshine is some crazy shit. And his dad brewed it himself? I have this mental image of a bathtub full of liquor, but I can't imagine that when I'm standing in Gabriel's spacious marble bathroom.

Scalding hot water turns my skin red. I don't remember much from last night. There was a phone call to Justin. Some memory of lying on the rug downstairs, though I don't know why. I feel between my legs, but there's nothing. I would feel something if he'd taken my virginity, wouldn't I? Some foreign texture, some soreness? The only ache I feel is in my head.

I stand under the wide showerhead forever, letting it beat away the last of my hangover. Then I get dressed in jeans and a T-shirt, because if he wants sexy, he'll have to supply the clothes himself.

I don't find Gabriel downstairs, though. Instead there's a heavyset woman whistling to herself as she kneads dough. She smiles when she sees me, her cheeks literally rosy. I'm not sure I've ever seen two perfectly round spots of color, but she has them. Flour coats her arms.

"Hello, Miss Avery. Are you hungry?"

As soon as she asks the question, my stomach

rumbles. I'm not entirely sure it should be trusted with food. That moonshine still lingers at the outer edges, threatening to make me dizzy. "Maybe a little."

"I can make you something. Eggs. Waffles."

I put my hands over my stomach. "I'm not sure."

She smiles sympathetically. "There's some Frosted Flakes in the pantry."

My eyes widen because I've always loved Frosted Flakes. They're simple and common, but they remind me of Sunday mornings with my dad. Our housekeeper had Sundays off, so we would dig through the pantry and watch cartoons. He would be on his phone half the time, but I didn't care.

How did Gabriel Miller know to stock Frosted Flakes for me?

How did he get a key to the house for the nurse?

How did he sign a consent form on my behalf for the agency?

He's breaking the law in a hundred different ways, and it's been less than twenty-four hours. But he's doing it to help me. Everything, designed to help me. That's more perplexing.

Before the auction he said that the buyer

would pay for a nurse so that he could have complete access to me. That the man would be rich enough that it wouldn't matter.

The Frosted Flakes aren't expensive. They don't give him more access to me, but they are thoughtful. Even sweet. And that matters more than I want to admit.

Without a word I head into the pantry and find a brand-new box of Frosted Flakes. I pour milk over it. With my bowl in hand I grab a seat at a rustic thick wood table.

The first bite makes my eyes close in pleasure.

"Mrs. Burchett," the woman says cheerfully. "And I'm to assist you in any way possible, so if you need anything, don't hesitate to holler."

She has a slight drawl that I can't quite place. "How long have you worked for Mr. Miller?"

"Oh, long enough to know that he wouldn't like me answering many questions."

I take another bite. She's undoubtedly right about that. "Where is he?"

She busies herself pressing the dough into a ceramic pie dish. "He had to go out. Business."

There's this hollow feeling in my stomach. I'm so used to fear, to the gnawing ache that's accompanied me ever since Dad was convicted, that I almost don't recognize it at first.

Disappointment. Except that doesn't make any sense. I don't want to spend time with Gabriel Miller. I don't want him to take my virginity. My memory from last night is hazy, but I think I'd feel some trace on my body if he'd had sex with me.

When I finish the cereal, I rinse out my dish.

"There's a television around the corner," she says. "Every show and movie you could want."

"Oh," I say, somewhat mystified by the idea of watching TV when I was purchased for sex.

"Or you could visit the library," she says, pulling out a covered bowl of what looks like chicken pot pie filling. I hope I'll be able to have some of that later.

She gives me directions, and I walk down the oversize hallways into an even larger room. My eyes widen as I realize this has a second floor, reachable by a spiral staircase. Little angels with trumpets are carved into the mahogany near the top. At the bottom, hands reach out of the flames.

Okay, that's disturbing.

What's even more disturbing is that this room seems made for me. The fire's already burning with a faint, pleasant crackle. There's a gleaming rustic wood chess set lined up in the center of the table.

On the table beside the fireplace are a stack of books—*Fairy Tales from around the Mediterranean, The Myth of Homer Revealed.* It's too much to think Gabriel spends his evenings reading Greek mythology. These are for me.

"Ready to play?" comes a low voice.

I whirl, dropping the book I'm holding. *Fairy Tales from around the Mediterranean* lands spread open, its spine stretched. I pick it up before it bends, hugging the large volume to my chest. "Play?"

He steps out from behind the spiral staircase. Was he waiting for me there? "Chess."

What would you do with her? Damon asked.

Play chess, Gabriel answered, turning me into a joke.

"No, thank you."

"Do you think you can say no?"

Defiance burns in my veins. My mind, my soul. That's my leverage, Candy said, and I don't plan to give him any. "You bought my body, that's all."

"I bought all of you."

"You can make me move around the pieces. Is that what you want?" An empty brainless automaton. That's all I'd give him, as plain as the actual pawn piece on the board. Chess is the game my daddy taught me, the game he played with me every week. And this is the man who ruined him. It would be a betrayal to play it with him.

He eyes the chess set with something like regret. "I'll leave you to your reading, then. I have some work to finish."

"Great," I manage, my voice tight.

I'm a little freaked out by Gabriel's uncanny knowledge of me. Justin got me a tennis bracelet for our last anniversary, shiny and bland. This is officially the sweetest thing anyone has ever done for me. From the man I hate the most.

Freaked out, but not enough to leave the room. I sit down and start to read.

Chapter Eighteen

FOR THE REST of the morning I manage to distract myself in the brutal poetry of the *Iliad*. There's war and famine, but it feels so far removed. I can get lost in the alien lands. When I stand up again, my back is stiff. I find a clear space on a rug in the corner, near the spiral staircase, and practice my yoga poses from memory. I'm wearing my favorite comfy jeans, soft but still restrictive in my movements. I manage the simple poses, though, to center my mind.

I'm feeling almost calm, considering the circumstances. Mrs. Burchett brings me lunch on a silvery tray. A wide slice of the chicken pot pie, pleasantly flaky on the outside, still bubbling on the inside.

It's only during the restless afternoon hours that I look up the Minotaur.

Every myth has some basis in fact, which is why the study of ancient history is so important.

Archeology can uncover some of the secrets. Myths whisper the rest of what we know. In that way myths provide more room for error and more room for discovery.

Ancient debts. War. Even human sacrifice. All of these have their roots in fact.

The Labyrinth was most likely the palace at Knosses, an elaborate architectural triumph that spanned six acres and climbed five stories. One thousand rooms probably accounted for the sense of a maze.

There are numerous pieces of evidence of human sacrifice on Crete, a morbid side of ancient mythology where I prefer not to dwell. Especially in light of my current situation.

It's the Minotaur himself who holds my fascination.

The child of Pasiphae, Minos's wife, who fell in love with a beautiful white bull. From their union came a child. A monster in every sense of the word, the Minotaur was banished to the Labyrinth and fed on sacrifice alone. Was the Minotaur some wild historical figure, distorted by the lens of superstition and poetry? Or was he the dark side of King Minos himself, the bastard child born of jealousy and greed?

These are the questions that plague me while I

curl up in the giant armchair, the fire growing dim. There's a slam from behind me—a door? A whoosh of wind sucks the air from the room. The faint flames from the log vanish, leaving me in darkness.

The book slides from my lap, hitting the rug with a thump.

I stand and whirl, facing the door. "Who's there?"

"Good evening," Gabriel says, strolling close.

I'm not sure when he became so familiar to me, but I can recognize his low voice without seeing him. I can make out his broad shoulders in the shadows. He tosses his jacket on the chair where I sat, and I catch a whiff of his masculine spice.

"What are you doing?"

"What I should have done last night. Tasting that…what was it he called you? The ripe peach?"

I take another step back, but there's a fireplace. The last dying embers. "Now?"

"I think a cherry would have been a better analogy, don't you?"

Having reached the end of the room, I walk sideways, circling, trying to keep the same distance away. He doesn't seem perturbed by my retreat. He doesn't slow at all.

"Wait," I say because I need to plan for this. I know he didn't have to give me last night. That was a reprieve I haven't earned, a night I already owe. I'm in his debt, but that doesn't mean I'm able to pay. "Just wait."

He laughs. "Almost twenty-four hours and I haven't touched you."

"You want to keep me a virgin," I say desperately, searching for anything to hold him back. I'm almost to the corner of the room now, on the soft rug with deep orange tones where I did yoga earlier.

"I didn't say I'd fuck you," he says, voice dark with promise. "I want to taste you."

Then it's too late to run. Too late to beg. He's standing right in front of me, and my back is to the stairs, wooden step digging into my calf. I can see him, scent him, but even stronger is the otherworldly *sense* of him, the presence that holds me frozen in front of him, thicker than chains.

"Taste me...where?"

One blunt finger lands on my lips. "I'll start here."

Then his lips are on mine, hot and soft and persistent. I'm helpless to his demands, opening to him, a sigh of acceptance drifting from my mouth to his. I know that everything happening here is inevitable, almost fated, but this part doesn't hurt. It feels almost like pleasure, his tongue swiping across mine, his teeth grasping my lower lip in carnal warning.

His hands cup my face, my neck. My breasts.

"Here," he says, his voice rougher.

Oh God, my breasts. I scramble back, but the stairs catch my feet. His hands grasp my shirt and yank, revealing me. My bra is pushed out of the way. There's no ceremony to the way he undresses me. It's not a striptease, it's a possession. He palms my breasts, feeling their weight.

"Smaller than they looked," he says, and I feel the flush creep over my chest.

I want to forget standing on that platform, being watched by so many men, but I know I never will. It's etched into my brain—the judgment and the lust, the shame and the control. "You bid on me." I know I sound defensive.

"It's not a complaint," he murmurs, pressing my nipple between his thumb and forefinger. "You're fucking glorious."

The unexpected compliment makes me blink. Then his mouth is covering my nipple, soothing away the burn, hot and eternal. He flicks me with his tongue, back and forth, back and forth, and I whimper with shock. My hand reaches out to grasp anything—and what I find is the carving of flames, of a hand reaching up out of the depths of hell. I'm burning.

He marks a path of openmouthed kisses over my chest, and I feel conquered. As if he's mapping every part of my body, owning me. What if he covers every inch? What part will be left for me?

His hot mouth closes around my other nipple, and my eyes fall shut. "Oh God," I whisper.

"That's right," he murmurs against me, the tease of his lips as he speaks unbearable. "Let yourself feel good."

There's a *though* in there—something about sacrifice. About pleasure. Why does he think I wouldn't let myself feel good? But then arousal arcs from nipples to my sex, and I forget about anything but his body over mine, his rough words promising so much more.

"Elbows on the steps," he says.

I can obey him without thinking. There's relief and shame, equal parts.

This position makes my breasts push out. I'm vulnerable like this, made into a living statue for him to touch and lick and suck. For him to bite, clasping my nipple between his teeth with a threatening growl.

"No," I moan. "Please."

His demonic laugh floats around me, as wild and effervescent as the moonshine from last night. I'm drunk on whatever he's doing to me, held captive by his desire.

Then his hand cups between my legs.

He squeezes. "And here."

I shake my head, because that's different. Kissing my mouth, my breasts. Those are one thing. What he's demanding is too intimate, and I fight him. He pulls at my jeans, and I twist away. His legs settle around me, locking my body against the stairs.

My hands clench the front of my jeans. "No, no. Not there."

"Elbows," he says. "Steps."

I cover myself for two breathless moments, shivering in doubt. Except I'm trapped against carved mahogany and muscled flesh. What choice do I have? I move my elbows back to the step behind me, pushing my breasts into his face. My cheeks flush in humiliation.

"Yes, sir," he says, his voice gentle.

"Yes, sir," I whisper.

His hands are clinical as they unbutton my jeans and pull down the zipper. He tugs off the jeans with a few rough pulls and tosses them aside. The panties go next. Maybe this part doesn't matter. He's seen it all before, and it's dark in the room. So dark with only the embers to wink at me from the fireplace.

Except I can't stop shaking, made so vulnerable by this position, by his command. Made naked by his very will. This is what it means to be owned by someone.

He pushes my legs apart. Not only a little, for him to touch me, for him to see. He pushes until the outsides of my legs touch the lip of the step. I'm completely exposed to him, spread open for him.

Blunt fingers nudge that slit—the one worth paying a million dollars for. Nothing's ever been inside there. Not a man. Not fingers. Not even a toy. He doesn't linger there but moves higher.

"Did you touch yourself?" he mutters.

I turn my face, looking at the black flames. "Yes."

"Like this?" he asks, pinching my clit between his thumb and forefinger. The same way he touched my nipple. It feels too rough at first, almost painful, until the heat turns to pleasure.

It's hard to talk when he's doing that. "Not like—more circles."

He draws a circle around my clit, and I buck into his hand. "Gabriel," I whisper.

"Right here," he says, voice as dark as the room. "I'm going to taste you right here, feeling your clit against my tongue, fucking you with my mouth until you cry. Do you want that, little virgin?"

I know the right answer, not only because he wants me to say it. Because I want him to do those things. *I want to live.* "Yes, sir."

He bends his head.

The first touch of his lips to my clit makes me jump. Only his large hands holding my hips keep me steady as he nibbles his way around my clit. He dips lower, a few large licks over my sex that have my toes curling against the wood.

"You don't taste sweet," he says, pausing. "You taste like I'm fucking dying and you're the only water around. You taste like goddamn air."

He puts his lips back on my sex, and I can't help the shrill scream that escapes me. God, what is he doing to me? I thought he might want me tonight—maybe we'd have dinner, some semblance of a date. Maybe he would come to my bedroom. I never expected to be caught in the library, to be spread open on the steps of a hand-carved staircase.

Every stroke of his tongue brings me higher, winds me tighter, until I'm rocking imperceptibly into his mouth. Little grunts escape me, matching the animalistic need in the air. I'm pushing against some cliff, held back by a barrier I don't understand, I can't name. I had an orgasm before, by my own hand, but this feels entirely different—a strange and uncontrollable beast.

I get close with a sharp whimper, and he slows his tongue, sliding down to my lips and back up again. My hand grasps his hair, pulling him where I need him. "Please."

"Do I need to tie you down?" he says, his voice thick. "I'd love to do that, little virgin. Remember what I said about fighting me."

"You'd enjoy it too much," I whisper, moving my elbows back to the stairs.

"Mhmm, and for that you'll have to wait. You'll have to wait until I'm done."

I groan because I'm right there, standing on the precipice, something sharp pressed into the breach. All I need is a few more glorious touches of his tongue. I'll burst. I know I will.

He pushes up from his kneeling position and pulls off his clothes. He's just as efficient, as unceremonial, as he was for mine. They're only fabric in the way of what he wants, shed quickly. Then he's standing there like some magnificent statue, like David, completely unselfconscious.

Unlike David, though, his private part juts out from his body.

He puts his fist around it. "Have you ever sucked a cock?"

I shake my head. "No, sir."

"Ever touched one?"

"No."

With his other hand, he grasps my hair and tilts my face up. "Have you ever seen a cock, little virgin?"

My eyes grow wide as I fight his hold on me. He tightens his fist in my hair until I squeak. "No, sir. I haven't."

"You're going to taste mine tonight, understand?"

One of his knees drops to the stairs near my elbow. He leans close, the tip of his cock an inch away from my lips. He pauses there, waiting. For what? I realize he wants me to meet him that final inch. He wants me to take control in this way— and I do, leaning forward to press a chaste kiss to the slick tip of his cock.

I hear his breath catch. "More, little virgin."

My tongue swipes the tip, the same way I felt his mouth on my clit.

He lets out a rough groan. "You're going to kill me."

There's wetness inside my mouth that came from him. It's thick and salty. "You taste like the sea."

"Fuck," he mutters, grasping my hair. This time he doesn't wait for me to meet him. Instead he holds me steady as his hips cant forward, pressing his cock into my mouth. He pushes past my lips, past the tip of my tongue, until my mouth feels unbearably full of him.

"You okay?" he says on a rough breath.

I look up at him and nod, my mouth still full.

Then he pushes forward, more than I thought was possible. The blunt end of his cock fills my throat, and my eyes water. My body fights him, trying to push him out of where he doesn't belong. He pulls back all on his own before thrusting in again.

His mouth on me felt invasive, but it's nothing like this. I'm pinned to the stairs by the thick length of him, made to taste him, breathe him. As he pulls back, the ridge of him swipes over my tongue, and a small spurt lands in my mouth. I roll it around my tongue like it's fine wine, as if I can sense what he's made of by the flavor of his sex. It's as complex as he is, as impenetrable and sharp.

He shoves back inside before I can fully drink

it down, and I swallow almost around him. He gives a hard sound of pleasure. "I want to be all the way inside," he mutters, sounding conflicted.

He isn't all the way inside? God, he would spear me to my core. I make a mumbling sound of panic, trying to shake my head with his hard length holding me still.

His laugh is unsteady. "I'll go easy on you."

If this is easy, I can't imagine what hard would be.

His hips find a pattern, the same one he teased me with on my clit. He pushes inside me, deep enough to feel my throat, before pulling out again. I get lost in the steadiness of it, like a ship being moved by the waves. There's no controlling it, no fighting. The only thing left to do is ride them. I let myself be tossed forward and back, pushed and pulled. Used.

He moves faster, his breath coming ragged. The sound of his need does something inside me, and I feel my inner muscles clench. It's strange that he can still touch my sex by fucking my mouth.

His roar begins low, almost a rumble. It ends with a sound of ferocity that reverberates through the library. I'm half-drunk on him, my mouth held open for his invasion. I wait for something that must come next—more of that salty flavor.

Instead he pulls back. I only have a moment to register the emptiness of my mouth, the ache in my jaw, before I feel the hot spray on my breasts. He paints my chest, my nipple. One high arc crosses my neck.

Blunt fingers push the come into my skin, rubbing it around. I feel impossibly marked. His. My skin tightens as he moves his seed over it. *His, his, his.*

His other hand reaches down to my clit, pinching hard. Fire overtakes me, flames licking my skin. I buck against his hand, making incoherent sounds, pleading. It's too much, too hard. Too good. He doesn't show any mercy, rubbing my clit with an intensity that wrings me out. My orgasm twists and twists, pulling tighter, until my muscles ache and my mouth is open in a silent scream.

CHAPTER NINETEEN

H E CARRIES ME upstairs, cradled in his arms like I'm something special. I know that I'm only here because he bid one million dollars. I know that he didn't come inside me only so that I would remain a virgin. Somehow I still feel safe in his arms, as if the pure force of his will can keep reality at bay. We're wrapped in something soft and pale, hidden from the world as he draws a bath and helps me inside. When I reach for the soap, he puts my hands on the curved edge of the tub. It's his square-tipped fingers and calloused palms that cover my body with soap. He cleans every part of me, soothing the abraded skin of my nipples, slipping between the slick folds of my sex. My eyes are only half-open. I'm still lost in that place he sent me when I climaxed, a place of pleasure, of peace.

When he's done, he helps me step out of the tub. A thick white towel dries me off while I stare at myself in the mirror. How many times have I showered before? How many times have the damp ends of my hair curled against my wet skin? Hundreds, thousands, and yet I look different. Still a virgin—by his definition. Different, though. A woman.

When he places me on the cool lavender sheets, I turn my face into the pillow and close my eyes. I'm expecting him to leave like he did last night.

The bed dips. He comes behind me, his arm slung over my waist, his legs tangling with mine. The heavy down comforter covers us both, and I can't help the sigh of gratitude.

"Go to sleep," he says, his voice low.

Something about the way he says it, I know he isn't going to sleep. So what is he doing here? Holding me? This isn't part of paid-for sex. It isn't revenge. Something else has his arm tightening around me, his face pressed into my half-damp hair.

"Thank you," I whisper.

He stiffens behind me. "Why would you say that?"

"It didn't hurt." More than that, it felt amazing. Soul restoring. After months of watching my life crumble around me, he built me back up. If only for a few minutes.

"Christ," he mutters, his hand clenching and releasing on my arm. "You deserve more than not hurting. Don't you get that? You deserve more than this."

I'm not sure I deserved to be sold like cattle, but I didn't deserve the fancy clothes, the best schools either. Life isn't about what you deserve, it's about making the best of what you have. And what I have is a strong, warm man holding me. "Then let me go."

He laughs softly. "I never claimed to do the right thing."

Maybe not right. That money would save me, though. Enough to save my father's house, to pay for his care after this month is over. Maybe enough to send me to college again. Did he think of all that when he spoke his bid aloud? Or had he only been concerned with winning? I'm not sure the distinction even matters, only the result.

I nestle deeper into his arms. "What did your father do? Besides make moonshine?"

"You mean petroleum? I can't believe you drank that stuff."

A flush comes to my cheeks as I remember the wild feeling of being drunk. "Was it like one hundred percent alcohol?"

"It was one hundred percent reckless," he

189

mutters. "You need to keep your defenses up with someone like me. That means staying sober, for starters. Sleeping with a knife under your pillow won't hurt."

I remember Candy's warning. *Your mind. Your soul. That's your leverage.*

Of course I hadn't asked—leverage against what? Maybe she just meant keeping my sanity, my dignity in the face of the auction. That's what I'd been worried about. Shame. Humiliation. But maybe she meant something worse. Something more treacherous. As if I should be on my guard. As if I'm in danger.

"You put me to bed," I reminded him. He'd had the perfect chance to hurt me then, when I would have been helpless to fight him, but he hadn't.

He doesn't say anything for a moment. "He was a liar. A thief."

I blink, realizing that he's telling me something true. Something precious enough that he wouldn't normally share it. "You hated him."

"I looked up to him, which was fucking stupid."

Every little boy looks up to his father. Little girls, too.

"You were a kid," I say, somewhat offended by his judgment of himself. I realize that there's a parallel between him and myself, but I choose not to follow that line of thinking.

"He never said anything that was true, almost as a matter of principle. He just conned as many people as he could meet, trying to get money so my mother could snort it, shoot it, drink it."

My stomach clenches. "She was an addict?"

"If you could get addicted, it was her favorite thing."

I swallow hard, glad he can't see the sympathy on my face. Harper's mother is an addict too. Most of the time she refuses to talk about it, but a few times, at night in our room at college, she would whisper in the dark about the fear, the dread. Hiding under the blankets at night while her mother was on a rampage, throwing everything in the house.

"I'm sorry for drinking your father's last moonshine," I say. "And if it bothered you to see me like that."

"I don't keep it to drink," he says gruffly. "I keep it to remember him. To remember what *not* to be."

A liar. A cheat. "That's why it bothers you so much when someone steals from you."

The reason he ruined my father. It wasn't only about setting an example for the rest of the criminal underworld. It was about setting an example for himself. About fighting back for every time his own father must have told him a lie.

It's King Minos who puts his bastard child into the Labyrinth. Not to kill him but to keep him locked away. The maze that Gabriel walks isn't a physical one, despite the large manor that he lives in. It's the emotional walls, the ones that make him strike out at people who get too close.

"And you're the furthest thing from an addict I've ever seen," he whispers.

The whole room seems to hold its breath with me. The thick carved bedposts, the sunny yellow stripes on the wall. Everything waiting. "What am I then?"

"You're innocent. And I'm going to ruin you." The certainty in his voice chills me.

Like he did my father. Except he stripped my father of his wealth, his power. And with this auction, Gabriel Miller is giving it back—to me.

In return he's going to take my virginity. Not tonight or the next night. Sometime in the next thirty days. And he believes it will be bad enough to ruin me. Worse than being penniless, worse than being shunned. Whatever he'll do to my body will be enough to break me.

You can have my body, I think. *But you can't touch my heart.*

CHAPTER TWENTY

W HEN I WAKE up, I'm alone.

I know it before I open my eyes, before I run my hand over the cool sheets behind me. It's in the air, a stillness. A loneliness that I was so used to it barely registered. Daddy tried to make space for me, but I still spent most of my time alone. And then after he was attacked, after I had to sell all the furniture, the house was achingly empty.

Even then I wouldn't have complained. It helped to smile when he was awake, to say that everything would be okay. Maybe I'd gotten so good at lying I was able to lie to myself, telling myself that I didn't really mind. That things would get better.

I could have kept on believing it except for those brief moments in Gabriel Miller's arms, those short and unexplainable moments when he'd held me.

No sex. No ulterior motives.

Not even money bound us together then. We were two people clinging together on a raft, the entire ocean spanning in every direction.

Then he woke up and left the raft, leaving me here.

I ignore the sense of disappointment, of loss, and step out of bed. The weather turned crisp in the past few weeks, but the floors of his house are heated. I curl my cold toes against the hand-scraped wood, seeking warmth. Always seeking warmth.

I don't bother to shower or tame my hair. I only throw on a shirt and some yoga pants, a complete morning mess. This is what he made me. And I have this urgent need to see him, to confirm that last night wasn't only a dream.

He's sitting at a desk, as if this is an ordinary morning. As if my axis didn't shift last night. As if his hands and his mouth and his cock didn't make me a woman.

He looks through papers on his desk despite the fact that I'm standing on the other side. Do people like him even have papers? My father used his printer quite a bit—his old eyesight never could get used to the screen. But Gabriel is younger than him, sharp enough to be fluent with technology. The file folder feels like a ruse.

"Gabriel."

He looks up briefly, his golden eyes merely a flicker of flame before he looks back down. "Yes, Ms. James."

Something inside me turns small and cold. I want him to call me Avery. *I want him to call me little virgin again.* "You left."

"I have work to do."

Present tense. It's not only an explanation as to why he left. It's a dismissal. Except that in yoga pants or a two-thousand-dollar Versace skirt, I'm Avery James. I was born and bred and goddamn raised to demand attention. I may not have deserved any of that privilege, but I don't deserve his scorn. "Can you at least look at me after I sucked your dick?"

That gets his attention. His gaze snaps to mine. He narrows his eyes, though I can't say he looks displeased. No, he looks hungry. Predatorial. He stands, and I take a step back.

"Yes, Avery. I tasted your pretty virgin cunt. You came against my fingers. Less than…"—he pretends to count—"twelve hours ago. Do you think I forgot?"

My chin lifts higher even as I take another step back. "You're acting like you did."

His steps are slow and graceful as he rounds

the desk. "I'm acting like a man who got what he paid for. Excellent service. Would you like a review on Yelp? Five stars."

I flinch. "Fine, push me away. Because you're scared of what happened."

"Scared?" he says, tasting the word. "I was taking it slow for you, little virgin. But if you're ready for more, I'll be sure to show you what scary things are waiting for you."

"Not sex. The way you held me after."

"You were shaking," he says, his voice almost soft.

"Have it your way," I say, my teeth gritted. "It's only sex between us."

"No, little virgin. It's only money between us." He reaches back to pick up the file folder. After a considering glance, he hands it to me.

It's like he's offering me a coiled snake, and I have to take it. I have to take it or I have to admit that I want there to be more between us than sex, than money. Of course I don't. Not with *him*. He ruined my father. He's a criminal. He goes against everything I believe in, but it would have been nice to have affection between us for the thirty days I'm here. Twenty-eight days, now.

I open the file folder, blinking at the stream of small black-and-white numbers. I've learned to be somewhat literate with investment accounts and bank statements since my father's attack. Lord knows I've learned how to read a bill. But I'm not sure what this is.

"An escrow account," he supplies. "It contains your percentage of the money from the auction."

My heart clenches. I stare at the paper as if I'm reading it, but I can't see anything. This is how I felt when the verdict came back guilty, when the call came from the cops about Daddy. When I sold the beautiful silver pendant with my mother's birthstone. An emerald. Daddy gave it to her the birthday before she died.

The file folder is clenched so tightly in my hand I'm surprised I'm not crushing it. Somehow I manage to close it and hold it at my side. My voice sounds hollow. "Thank you."

He said there's only money between us, but he's a fucking liar. In the air there's rage and revenge, betrayal and lust. I may be innocent, as he called me, but I know what I feel.

"You're excused," he says, his voice hard. "I'll call for you when I want you."

Like I'm some kind of servant. Like I'm a *maid,* brought in to clean whenever he makes a mess. Like I'm a maid for his *cock,* barely a warm body to wipe himself.

Chapter Twenty-One

I T'S FINE, I tell myself. It's better this way.

Because if I don't have my lies, what will I have left? Gabriel reminded me where I stand with him. Someone to serve him, something he purchased. I can keep him at a distance regardless of what he does to my body, as long as he doesn't cradle me close like I'm something worthwhile again.

I should be focused on Daddy, anyway. He's the reason I'm doing this. I call Mr. Stewart at the nursing home using his personal cell phone. He assures me that my father is in excellent health, which seems like it must be a lie until he conferences in the day nurse.

"Hello, pumpkin." My father's voice sounds rusty, tired, but undeniably aware.

"Daddy? Are you okay?"

"I'm working on getting better." He gives a hoarse laugh. "They've got some good meds hooked up. And there's this devil of a physical therapist coming every day now. I've called him every name in the book, but I managed to sit up on my own yesterday."

My breath catches. "Are you serious?"

"Don't you worry about me. You focus on your studies."

With a sinking heart I realize he thinks I'm at school. "Oh. Right."

When Mr. Stewart comes on, I can't help the strange sadness that creeps into my voice. "He sounds great."

"It's very common," he says, his voice sympathetic. "We see it all the time. Family wants to tend to their own, but it's a huge burden, a constant stress, and all without the necessary training. Our nutritional counselor has worked with a private chef to develop meals that are best for him. And the physical therapist is our very best."

Somehow that makes me feel worse, even though I know that doesn't make sense. I was killing myself making sure my father's meds were right, that his IV was right, that he was comfortable and clean. And it had all been making him worse because I didn't know what the hell I was doing. These trained people know what they're doing. And the only way I can afford them is by fucking Gabriel Miller.

Only after I hang up do I see the string of increasingly urgent texts from Harper.

> *It's me. What's going on??*
>
> *Justin just called me. He might have cried. He's very drunk. CALL ME.*
>
> *Were you in an auction? Type OMFG for yes or n for no.*
>
> *Pigeons. Flags. Letter in a bottle. All acceptable forms of communication in this FUCKING EMERGENCY.*

I have to laugh at the last text, because it's so perfectly Harper. And it's a laugh-or-cry situation, realizing that Justin found out exactly what I've done.

And apparently he's sharing the news.

I'm ruined in Tanglewood. Of course I knew that from the moment I accepted Damon Scott's proposition. Even if somehow the auction remains a dirty little secret, I can't face the wealthy upper crust of the city ever again.

But I hoped it would be contained. Like a tiny explosion under a metal dome in a cartoon. Boom! And all that's left is scorch marks in the shape of a circle.

Except if Justin knows, if Harper knows, then

the circle is spreading. I don't think Harper is going to gossip about me, but shit like this is wildfire. All it has to do is spark to the next tree to keep going.

She answers on the first ring. "Tell me everything, starting from the very beginning."

Debt. Bills. An auction and a million dollars in escrow. I tell her everything, because I'm desperate for some advice here. "So that's the story of how I became Smith College's first hooker."

She snorts. "You're definitely not the first, but that's a story for another day. Now you need to tell me about this Gabriel Miller motherfucker. Is he old? Mean? Has a gold tooth?"

I smile. "Not exactly. He's actually…"

I'm not sure how to describe his golden eyes, how they can pierce me from across the room. How can I explain the way his broad shoulders and large hands make me feel delicate? "He looks okay. That's not the problem."

"Uh-oh," she says. "Angry wife?"

"God, you are the most jaded. No, he's not married." At least I don't think he is. "He's the man who turned my father in. Who gave all the evidence to the attorney general so they could prosecute."

"Oh my God. A do-gooder?"

"It was a revenge thing. My father cheated him."

"Thank God," she says, sounding relieved.

"No, we're not thanking God. Because he hates me."

"He hates your dad."

"He hates my *family*. And he's already ruined my dad. Money. Reputation. Even physically. In every way possible my father has lost everything."

"Except his beautiful daughter."

I wince. "Something like that."

"And you think he just bought you to get back at your dad."

My fingers trace lavender flowers carved into the bedpost. "I don't know what he's thinking. Is buying me revenge enough or does he have something worse planned?"

"Worse, like...sex. The auction was two days ago, right?"

"Right, but he hasn't done that yet."

"He hasn't touched you?" She sounds incredulous.

"He's touched me." I feel my cheeks flame with the memory of his touch, the memory of his tongue. "But he hasn't taken my virginity. And the way he talks about it...it scares me. Like he's planning to make it awful. Is that crazy?"

I want her to tell me that's crazy, that a man like Gabriel Miller wouldn't resort to that. That it would be too cruel, too kinky, too *something* to be real.

"It makes sense," she says, musing. "How much did your dad steal from him?"

"I don't know." A lot. More than I can ever repay, even with the money from the auction—which came from him, anyway. "And it's more the principle of it. He has a thing about people who lie."

"Really? Well, do you think you can get him to talk? If he has a thing about lying, he might be honest with you."

I'm not sure if it would be better or worse to know he has something awful planned for me. "I can try. But look, I need you to be honest with me. People say it hurts, the first time. Does it?"

"I think everyone is probably different," she says, but she's hedging.

"Harper."

"My first time was with the gardener. I was fourteen. He was nineteen."

I wince because I didn't know that about her. It's a pretty big age difference. "Wow."

"I bled so much my mom gave me this awkward talk about what periods are while she was stoned out of her mind. I didn't have the heart to tell her that I'd gotten my period a year ago."

My heart clenches. "Oh, sweetie."

"Here's what I think you should do. When you think he's going to do it, take a pill. Or have a drink. Something to dull the edge, you know?"

Despite my growing fear of actual penetration, I crack a smile. "I already tried that. The first night. He ended up tucking me into bed."

"That's pretty sweet for a motherfucker."

"Yeah." My smile fades. "He can be sweet one minute. Then the next he's dismissing me from the room, telling me he'll call me when he wants to use me. His actual words: use me."

She makes an outraged sound. "Who does he think he is?"

"My owner." At least for the next twenty-eight days.

Chapter Twenty-Two

I DON'T HAVE to wait long to find out when he plans to use me.

After my phone call with Harper, I leave my room and wander the large hallways, peeking into empty rooms as if one of them will hold the key to unlock Gabriel Miller. As if he's storing all his secrets in some kind of trophy room, ideally with neon arrows and handy signage to point me in the right direction.

All I find are endless corridors of comfortable, expensive rooms—sitting rooms, bedrooms. How many people can this place actually hold? There's also a movie room with three small rows of leather chairs and a screen that takes up an entire wall. A large gym with a sauna attached. There's even a small art gallery on the top floor featuring some estate pieces, some local artists, and a particularly gorgeous Sargent painting of a woman by a piano.

I manage to avoid his office, the open door allowing his voice to carry as he speaks on the phone.

Only one room is a mystery. Locked.

The brass knob doesn't turn. The rooms were filled with antique furniture and sculptures. Even the priceless paintings in the art gallery hadn't been locked.

At the end of my exploration I don't know that much more about Gabriel than when I started. And my feet are aching. It takes me another fifteen minutes before I can even find my room.

When I get there, I see a tray with lunch and another note scrawled in his square, careless script.

We're going out at seven. Your clothes are in the closet.

I feel like I'm on a scavenger hunt as I peek into the closet. Hanging in front of my clothes is a black vinyl bag, floor-length. I zip it open and gasp. A stunning Oscar de la Renta dress made of some kind of white sheer fabric, layered to produce a wide skirt that ends midcalf. Flecks of gold center around the waist, making the whole thing look like a sculpture. And that's when it's still flat in the bag. I can only imagine how it will look when it's on.

On a little island in the closet there's a black box that contains champagne-gold peep-toe

Jimmy Choos. A small velvet box contains a delicate gold bangle inlaid with pearl.

Mercy.

Daddy was always generous with my allowance. And I realized from a young age that my appearance reflected on him. If I showed up at a society event in a clearance-rack dress, everyone would whisper that he must be struggling. Until six months ago I was able to walk into any store and pull out my American Express.

This dress, though. It isn't the kind of dress that you can buy off the rack. This is a dress that you need a connection to get. A connection and very large sums of money.

This is a red-carpet dress.

Where the hell is he taking me?

At seven o'clock sharp he knocks on my bedroom door. I spent the past hour putting makeup on and taking it off, thinking it's too much or too little. I need Candy to prepare me for this, but she was only my fairy godmother for the ball. I have to figure this out for myself.

I settled on thick loose curls for my hair and a classic red lipstick.

When I open the door, he does this little shake of his head as if he can't believe what he's seeing. It's the dress of course: subtle yet stunning, intricate yet simple. Even knowing that, I can't help the blush that colors my cheeks.

He pauses, taking me in from head to toe. "The dress suits you."

"Thank you." Of course he looks ridiculously handsome in a tux that was no doubt tailored to him, but I'm not going to admit that. "You're looking sharp."

He gives me the barest of smiles. "I try."

"Where are we going?"

It's wrong to be excited about this. *It isn't a date!* I have to keep reminding myself of that, because it feels like one. Especially when he says, "We could go downstairs and play a match."

Chess. Leverage. There's a strange longing to play with him, to wear the prettiest dress I've ever worn while I play my favorite game in a beautiful library. That would be the perfect date. With the wrong man.

I'd give anything to play another game with my daddy.

Gabriel made sure that would never happen again. No, he's not getting my mind. He paid for my body. I shake my head.

"Ah," he says as if that was expected. "In that case, we'll go to the theater."

Oh, I love the theater. I manage not to

bounce on my heels. "What are we seeing?"

"*My Fair Lady.*"

The story is based on Pygmalion, the myth of a sculptor who fell in love with his art. The gods granted him his wish, turning marble into flesh. "I didn't realize it was touring."

His expression seems brooding. Does he see the symmetry between us? The man with all the power. The woman made real by his love for her? Of course he doesn't love me. And more importantly, he isn't changing me in any way. *Except sexually.*

"Opening night," he says.

My stomach drops. Opening night. A regular theater night, it would be easy to get lost in the crowd of people. We would find our seats, the lights would lower. We'd watch the show side by side in the dark. But opening night is another beast entirely. Usually the seats are claimed by season pass holders, if there are any left after the high level donors have claimed theirs. Or they make them available for a higher price, invite only, with the proceeds going to charity. However it's done, a few things hold true: only the most rich and powerful people will be attending. And there will most definitely be drinks and mingling before the show starts.

He isn't taking me to the theater so that we can enjoy ourselves. This isn't a pretend date where we both act like he isn't paying for the pleasure of my company. This is a show, an example, as surely as my father's demise. I'm going to be put on display, a bird in a gilded cage.

"I see," I say, my voice flat.

He looks almost regretful. "You'll do fine."

His pity burns like acid. If I have to be trapped in this cage, if I'm going to be forced to sing, I'm going to sound beautiful doing it. Somehow I smile. "Of course."

I hold his arm as he escorts me downstairs, as if I'm not heading to the guillotine. I find a bland expression for the limo ride to the theater, as if my heart isn't beating a million times a minute. There are going to be so many people there. The men Daddy was friends with. They all know what Gabriel Miller did to my father. What will they think about seeing me with him?

Some of them will know about the auction.

Then a worse thought strikes me. Some of them could have attended the auction.

CHAPTER TWENTY-THREE

T HE WHISPERS START as soon as we walk into the room.

They follow us as we pause for pictures at the step and repeat backdrop at the end of the carpet—not actually red but purple instead. They follow us up the grand staircase. They follow us to the drink station where Gabriel asks for a glass of champagne for me and a whiskey neat for himself.

"I could have wanted a whiskey," I mutter, more because I need to fight back. And I can't yell at the old women to stop pointing at me, can't scream at the men to stop staring at my ass.

"I've seen you drunk," Gabriel says mildly. "No whiskey."

Yes, and that's probably not something we need to repeat in public. I can't deny that I'd love some oblivion right now, though, because I see several of my father's friends approaching. One owns a large housing development corporation, the other a manufacturing plant for tampons, of all things. I only ever see them together. Daddy played poker with them all the time.

They smile genially as the bartender finishes our drinks. "Miller! Great to see you here."

Gabriel hands me a flute, and I take a fortifying sip—then scrunch my nose as the bubbles tickle me from the inside. I hear the amusement in Gabriel's voice as he says, "You too, Bernard. How's work been treating you?"

"Very stiff," he says solemnly. "But we have plans to expand."

Do not laugh, Avery. I manage to keep a straight face as he turns to me.

"And how has school been treating you? Are you still on leave to help your father?"

Technically my absence is being recorded as leave by the school, but everyone knows I have no means to go back. And I'm standing here beside Gabriel Miller, which shows exactly how academic my life has become. Even the auction won't be enough to send me back to Smith College, once the house and my father's caregivers are covered.

"Yes," I say, keeping my voice polite and distant. "He's doing very well."

"Good, good," the other man says. "I hope we can resume our poker games soon."

I want to punch him in the face, because it's

clearly a lie. He was one of the first men to stop answering Daddy's phone calls once the scandal broke. And even if Daddy were able to sit upright at a poker table, he wouldn't have anything to gamble. This is the kind of bullshit that I always hated, but it strikes a little harder when it's directed at my family.

"Of course," I say, teeth clenched. Apparently that's become my go-to answer when what I really want to say is *go to hell, asshole.*

Gabriel smiles as if he knows exactly what I'm thinking. "If you'll excuse us, gentlemen. There's something I want to show Ms. James."

A firm hand on my lower back guides me deeper toward the atrium. We're not even two feet away when I hear those bastards snickering about the things Gabriel Miller is going to *show* me.

"I hate them," I whisper, tears stinging my eyes.

Gabriel pulls me along, his voice almost droll as he adds, "Fucking brownnosers."

I glance at him in surprise. "I thought they were your friends."

"They're not anybody's friends. If your father thought otherwise, that was his mistake."

My jaw clenches hard because he's right. I

hate that he's right.

Damon Scott breaks from a group of men and lopes over to us, all casual confidence. He's wearing a different three-piece suit, this one with tiny gold fleurs-de-lis stitched into the blue fabric. "Good evening. And here I thought to worry about you, Ms. James. But you look radiant."

Radiant? I manage a thin smile. "Thank you."

Damon leans close. "How is Gabriel treating you? Tell me honestly."

The sparkle in his eye says it's more filthy curiosity than concern for me. Gabriel makes a low growling noise that has Damon chuckling. They're sharks, I realize. Sharp teeth. A taste for blood. And I'm wounded.

"Is Candy here?" I ask, hoping Ivan Tabakov likes the theater. I could use more of her advice. These men might be sharks, but she's learned how to tame them.

"No," Damon says with a smirk. "I think this is past her bedtime."

A woman waved to Gabriel—a tall and leggy blonde I didn't recognize. I wanted to think her makeup was trashy or her dress too revealing, but she looked perfect. I hated that Gabriel gave us a curt, "Excuse me a moment," before going to speak with her.

I tried not to shoot daggers with my eyes. I had no right to be jealous. No *desire* to be jealous. This was a business arrangement, however cold that felt.

"So how is he really treating you?" Damon asks, his voice mild.

"Fine," I say tightly, pretending not to watch the way the woman touches Gabriel's arm. I look up at the balcony instead, catching a few people staring at me.

"Don't tell me I need to ride to your rescue. I'd hate to have to return my percentage of the money. And my armor is all rusty."

My laugh feels raw, my eyes strangely stinging. "No, I'm fine. I guess I should thank you. If you hadn't done all that I'd have lost my family's house."

He ducks his head, looking almost boyish. "I'd say anytime, but I guess we already popped the cork on that champagne bottle."

A startled laugh bursts out of me. What a comparison. If I had to be champagne at least I'm a bottle of Moët et Chandon, the kind Daddy got for my graduation party.

Of course, technically the cork hasn't popped.

My cheeks heat with the realization. "Right."

"I have to admit I was a bit nervous when Gabriel suggested the auction. And definitely when he bid on you. But it seems like it's working out."

Why was he nervous about me with Gabriel? Another head turns in my direction, only to quickly look away when we make eye contact. "Everyone's staring at me."

He scans the room. "To be fair, they'd do that for anyone on Gabriel's arm."

"But they know. At least some of them have to know about the auction. So many people were there. And that's not even counting the pictures."

He quirks a brow. "Pictures?"

"You know, the pictures you took to generate interest for the auction. The photographer at the Den."

There's a long pause where he looks quizzical. He speaks slowly, thoughtfully. "There weren't any pictures, Ms. James. Gabriel said you bailed on him, that you couldn't go through with the shoot. Is that true?"

My heart thuds, a worried beat. Why did he lie? No one saw those pictures. I try to keep the relief from my face. No one except for Gabriel Miller. "Yes."

The corner of his mouth turns up. "No, I guess I'm not worried about you."

Just then Gabriel returns to us, his mouth set

in a hard line.

Damon takes the opportunity to slip away, giving us a jovial wave. "Now I have more people to talk to, more men who desperately want to part with their money."

He strides away, waving to another group of people. He's clearly using this evening for business. Is that what Gabriel is doing? Except he doesn't seem interested in talking to anyone but me. *And he lied about the pictures.*

"If you want to mingle, you don't have to take me along," I say.

He cocks his brow. "Why would I want to mingle?"

"I don't know. Business." A shrug. "For the same reason Damon's here."

"He's here because he's lusting after a certain dancer in the show. And I don't do business at the theater."

"Where do you do business, then? A back alley?"

As soon as the words leave my lips, I wish I could take them back. That's not an arrow I meant to fling. And no one gets away with insulting Gabriel Miller like that.

He laughs softly. "What makes you think I'm a criminal?"

But then this is Gabriel Miller, who values honesty above everything. And I remember what Harper told me, that he would be honest with me too. He might evade the question, he might refuse to answer, but whatever he said would be the truth.

"You're friends with Damon Scott."

"Ah, that."

"And you're a member of the Den."

"A founding member, actually," he says. "But your father did business with me. How bad can I be?"

His tone is blithe because we both know that my father was involved in a lot of underhanded dealings. I'd never have guessed it, but it all came out in court. The bribes, the dummy corporations. God. Of course Gabriel Miller managed to keep his name completely out of court documents, only supplying the evidence that the prosecutor needed to begin his investigation.

I take a step forward, moving out of range of his hand. Then I turn to the window, looking out over the city. A storm has crept across the skyscrapers, catching the spires and stair-step slopes in its gray net. It will be raining by the time we leave.

"I buy and sell things," he finally says. "Like

most businesses do."

"What kind of things?"

"Other businesses, mostly."

But not entirely. "Drugs. Guns?"

"If the money is right, anything is for sale."

"People?"

"I bought you, didn't I?"

His presence is warm and solid behind me, making sure I don't escape. Or keeping everyone else away? I'm not sure, but I know that he's not here to make my life easier. He's here to use me, exactly as he said he would. To show everyone how low my father has fallen, that even his daughter is ruined.

"What did my father buy from you, anyway?" I say, bitterness tinging my voice.

"I bought something from him, actually."

I turn in surprise, forgetting to hide my face. "You did?"

I never knew the details of the transaction that ruined everything. That wasn't part of the court case. But it was common knowledge in the city. Gabriel made sure of that.

"His shipping company. It was failing, and he was looking for a buyer. I met with him a few times. My lawyers met with his. We made an offer. He accepted."

My eyes widen. "No."

Daddy owned several businesses, but his international shipping business was the largest one. His bread and butter. The bulk of his wealth. It had been in trouble, even before the mess with Gabriel Miller? I don't want to believe that, because he should have told me. I should have known.

Gabriel watches the clouds, his golden eyes reflecting the rolling darkness. "Only after the papers were signed did I find out he had secretly sold off the company's most valuable assets to other holding corporations, thus rendering my purchase almost worthless."

My mouth drops open. Nothing Daddy did should surprise me anymore, but somehow it still does. After all the lectures he gave me about integrity and family pride. After the chili juice on my fingers. I had come to see him as ten feet tall, some kind of paragon of morality.

"How?" I manage.

He shrugs. "A dollar sale here. Twenty-five cents for million-dollar property there. He's not the first man to try and cheat me. He won't be the last, though less will try now that they've seen what happens."

I swallow hard because I don't want to think of how many lives were ruined. "There wasn't anything you could do?"

His smile looks feral, more like a snarl. "Oh, there were plenty of options. I could have contested the deal in court—and won."

"Why didn't you?"

"It wouldn't have been enough. I could have had him killed for what he did."

My stomach tightens. Someone almost killed him one night, but they left him alive.

He continues, "Death would have made him a martyr, though. I wanted him alive. Alive and suffering, so that everyone in the city would see what happens to someone who fucks with Gabriel Miller."

"Is that why you brought me here?" We both know the answer is yes.

He smiles faintly. I see the reflection in the window, overlaid on the stormy clouds. "You play chess. Surely you know the many uses of a pawn."

I flinch because I know exactly what I am to him. It's my role in this game: to fall when the time is right, to protect the king until I've run out of time.

To sacrifice myself at the perfect turn.

"The city is beautiful like this, held down by the sky," he murmurs.

But when I glance at his reflection, it's not the city he's looking at. It's me.

Chapter Twenty-Four

ANY HOPE OF escaping the spotlight fades when he leads me up the stairs, away from the mezzanine seating and toward the boxes. Our seats give us a perfectly clear view of the stage, a drama lover's dream. Unfortunately they also give everyone in the theater a perfect view of us. I pretend not to see people craning their necks to look at us.

Gabriel is every inch the gentleman as he waits for me to sit in the plush velvet chair before taking his seat beside me. The lights dim, but that doesn't mean the whispering stops. I can feel their curious gazes crawling over my skin.

That's kind of the point.

I may as well have my wrists in metal chains rather than a golden bangle. He might as well grab my hair and drag me around rather than lead gently with a hand at the small of my back. That's how clearly he's subjugating me in front of everyone. That's how strong the message is. He owns me.

He made it clear that he's my enemy, if I still had any doubt. I'm the pawn, and he's my triumphant captor. And yet there are those moments of tenderness that I can't quite turn away from. Drops of water that I'm thirsty enough to drink.

Like the pictures he hadn't given to Damon Scott to share.

The play captures my attention from the first song, and I'm soon lost in the aching distance between Eliza and Henry. She's brash and beautiful, her accent both foreign and endearing. Of course he strips her of it, attempting to turn her into a more desirable woman. And so comes to desire her. Except what remains of the woman that she had been? If you have to change to be loved, then how much is that love worth?

I don't know who would be my Professor Higgins—Justin, who wanted the perfect society wife? Or Gabriel Miller, who wants a sexual slave?

In the end neither one of them fit the bill, because neither of them love me. They can want me, they can fuck me. But they don't love me.

The curtain falls for intermission.

Gabriel stands and holds out his hand. "Come. I did have something to show you earlier."

I bite back a hundred sarcastic comments—that I would just as soon not be strutted around like a trophy he's won, that I have no interest in seeing what he's packing. Instead I place my hand in his.

This time when he leads me into the atrium, he ignores the hands that rise in his direction as people try to speak to him. This time he doesn't let me turn away to the window.

I gasp when I see it, only the top right corner of oil on canvas.

As we get closer I read the placard standing at the velvet rope. A painting by Jean-Leon Gerome of Pygmalion and Galatea, on loan from the Met for opening night only. I forget for a moment that I despise Gabriel Miller and his public ownership of me.

"Can we go in?"

Amusement dances in his eyes. "I thought you might refuse to come with me for intermission."

Because I thought he wanted to do something dirty. Not *this*. "Please."

He nods at the attendant, who unhooks the chain on the velvet rope. As we enter, the crowd clears out almost immediately. I'm not sure why we're allowed to look at the painting almost exclusively, even for a moment, but I'm not going to question it.

There's security on either side of the painting, no doubt required by the museum. But they're standing at a distance, outside the ropes. Right beside the painting is a woman in chino slacks and a white button-down shirt. It's a somewhat casual dress for the opening night, but it's clear from her stance, her hands in her pockets, that she isn't a guest. She's here to speak about the painting, but she isn't a docent.

"Hello," she says kindly. "Please let me know if you have any questions."

I want her to tell me everything. "Can you tell me about the provenance?"

Her eyes light up as she describes the creation of the painting by Gerome—a series of paintings, actually, each viewing Pygmalion and his statue embracing from a different angle. It was purchased from the artist in 1892 by a dealer who then sold it to a private entity in the United States, where it remained until 1905.

"Why did he make so many paintings?" I hadn't known about the paintings, actually. I only knew about his sculptures.

"He believed it was a hackneyed subject, Pygmalion and Galatea. He wanted to revive them, to find something new about them. All of the paintings focus on the moment when she comes to life."

"So he was painting his sculpture?"

She smiles. "You know he sculpted her too?"

I flush, because a year ago I would have mentioned that I'm majoring in ancient mythology. Now I'm just a girl who used to read a lot of books. "Mythology's an interest of mine."

From her pants pocket she produces a business card. "Mine as well. If you'd like to chat about it, you can always shoot me an e-mail."

My eyes widen as I read the card. *Professor of Classics* at the state university. "Wow."

Her shrug is somehow not modest at all, which is endearing. "My focus is more on the ancient history represented in the painting, rather than nineteenth century European art."

I feel unbearably hungry for any knowledge she can give me. I went from a waterfall of intellectual stimulation in college to a veritable desert in a large empty house. "What are you working on now?"

"I just got back from Cyprus actually. Studying the moss in Nicosia for clues about diet and disease in ancient times. We're still working through the samples in the lab."

"You're my new favorite person," I say, clutching the card like it's a lifeline. "I'm going to write you. And look you up and read every paper you've ever written."

She laughs. "I have a few stacks of journals in my office I could give you if you're interested."

"I'd sell my soul for them," I say, fairly seriously. I try not to think about the fact that I've already sold my soul—or at least, my body—for one million dollars. Or the fact that the buyer is standing two feet behind me, watching the entire exchange.

Is he silently laughing at me, like the men at the auction? As if all my curiosity, my accomplishments are a big joke for the men around me?

And I can't even argue the point, because I'm the one on the platform. I'm the one for sale.

The professor launches into a story about her coworker's unfortunate encounter with a wild goat during their last trip, and I'm distracted from my own disgrace.

CHAPTER TWENTY-FIVE

A S WE'RE HEADING up the stairs, I realize he's taking a different path to the box. Except we're not heading toward the box anymore.

"Gabriel?"

He pushes open a door to a dark room and turns to face me. "After you?"

My eyes are wide as I take in the strange shapes of shadows inside. Props. This is some kind of storage room for theater equipment. We aren't supposed to be in here. And there's only one reason Gabriel Miller would want to take me somewhere private.

There's a tremble reserved only for *him,* only for sex. I know it's going to happen between us. A thousand different positions, a million different ways. And all of that before he even takes my virginity, strictly speaking. Knowing it's inevitable doesn't take away the fear. How much will it hurt? How much will he *make* it hurt, on purpose, to humiliate me?

"Inside, little virgin."

He has infinite patience even though intermission only lasts for fifteen minutes. How many did we spend at the painting? Five minutes? Ten? He doesn't look rushed, though. He looks like a man assured of his power, a king standing at the back of the board while his subjugates fight the war.

I step inside, breathing in the scent of cedar and linen. And something else, something metallic. Maybe rust. There's a collection of strange things in this room. I can make out the shape of an oak tree in the corner, its limbs spreading wide. On the other side there's a row of bleachers, like a high school football game would have. A Native American tepee and a lemonade stand.

Gabriel closes the door, draining even that faint bit of light.

He stands behind me, a solid presence. Unyielding.

"No stairs this time," I whisper.

He moves me as if he can see in the dark. I'm blind, blinking into the blackness, dust stinging my eyes. God, what if we run into something? What if we trip and fall? But his hands guiding my arms are firm and sure, his movements focused on a single goal.

When I finally feel something plush and unmoving hit the front of my thighs, he stops. A large hand covers my back. Then he pushes me forward. I'm bent over something rounded. My hands feel smooth leather and tufted buttons. A sofa. The sloping kind that a psychiatrist would use.

My ass is in the air, completely vulnerable to him, something that becomes painfully clear when he flips up my dress. Large hands smooth over my panties before tugging them down.

This is happening so quickly, too quickly. My breathing comes faster and faster. The dust fills my lungs. I'm going to suffocate like this. *Oh God.*

"Breathe," he says, his hands stroking my sides.

I'm a horse and this is my flank. It's embarrassing how well it works, how easily I calm under his touch. Some people have that effect, I've heard. Some instinct that tells us we can trust them. My very own virgin whisperer.

Except that instinct is a lie. This man bought me at auction for one purpose only: to break me.

My breathing has calmed, and I lay my cheek against the cool leather.

"That's right," he murmurs. "This isn't going to hurt. So afraid of pain, aren't you? Why do you always expect the worst, little virgin?"

Because you're a monster!

Is he, though? The time on the spiral staircase didn't hurt. Maybe every time will be like that—intimate and filthy. And pleasurable, yes. He made me climax so hard I felt it for hours. All night long.

He's saving my virginity for last, though. And like he said, I play chess. I know how to move the pieces around the board, plotting and planning for the final strike. How to lull your opponent into a false sense of security. Or like he so eloquently put it: how to use a pawn. It will hurt in the end. That's the only way he wins. And a man like Gabriel Miller never loses.

He runs his hand over my bare ass, gentle and sure. "The chili juice. That one really did a number on you, associating sex with pain." He gives a rough laugh. "And I thought I was kinky."

I flinch in the dark, because what Daddy did wasn't kinky. It couldn't have been kinky, because it involved his daughter. He did it to me. "He was trying to protect me."

Two fingers slip between my legs, seeking the wetness between my folds. "And how did that work out?"

Horribly, since he's now pinching my clit. I

press my lips together, fighting back a moan. But his fingers are relentless and skillful, playing me until I'm panting, whimpering. "Oh my God!"

"That's right," he whispers. "It doesn't have to hurt. All you have to do is give in."

I can't give in. Giving in means living in the Labyrinth, losing, *dying* here. It means letting go of the string that's my only way out. Maybe the chili juice did mess me up. The masturbation. Waiting until marriage. But since the auction it's been Gabriel Miller messing with my mind, making me want things I shouldn't. "Please."

"I ought to spank you for this, for fighting me."

"I'm not fighting," I say, my jaw tight. Of course he's right. I'm fighting him, but not with punches or kicks. I'm fighting to maintain hold of my sanity.

"You'd like that, wouldn't you? A spanking? I could bruise you for days. Then you could paint me as the big bad wolf." I hear a zipper from behind, but his hand on my clit doesn't pause. "I'll just have to make you come instead."

A chime sounds from far away, signaling that intermission is almost over.

"We have to go," I gasp out, pushing to get up.

He doesn't even have to hold me down. It's only his fingers on my clit that keep me pinned to that sofa. It's merciless, the way he circles them. Not too hard, not painful. He knows that wouldn't work. Instead he's patient, endlessly patient, while my body winds tighter and tighter. All my muscles clench, bearing down on the arm of the sofa, rocking against his hand. I want this despite myself, and his low baritone laugh tells me that's the point.

I feel something else, a rocking motion in time with my own. His hand, I realize. He's jerking himself off. At the same time that he circles my clit, the same tempo. *It will be like this when he's inside me.*

Even then I can't come, my body tearing itself apart. It hurts like this, and I'd rather come just to finish it. My muscles are spasming, mouth open on a helpless, silent scream.

"Come, little virgin," he says, his voice choked.

There's a splash of something hot on the backs of my thighs. *His come.*

The orgasm overtakes me like a tidal wave, turning me upside down, filling my nose with saltwater, making everything dark blue and blurred. I tumble with no idea which way the surface is, my lungs burning with the need to breathe.

When I break the surface, Gabriel has collapsed on top of me. He pants into my hair, muttering, "Jesus. Jesus."

My hands are fists against the leather, which is slick with our sweat. The smell of sex scents the air, like ocean water and dark spice. We remain molded together like clay, breathing together, coming back to life together.

He pushes up and uses something—a hand-kerchief?—to wipe his come from my legs. Even when I stand, I can feel the hardening residue of him there. I'm marked.

There's only a few frantic seconds to pull up my panties and push down my skirt.

Then he's opening the door.

I emerge like some newborn deer, unsteady on my legs, blinking at the blinding sun after being in the womb. I would have collapsed on that thin magenta carpet except for his hand around my waist, his other under my elbow.

We pass a man, and I duck my head, trying not to meet his eyes.

Until I hear his voice sounding strangely familiar. "Well, Gabriel. Look at you making good use of your purchase."

I look up to see the gray-haired man who'd

had a beautiful blonde on his arm at the auction. Today it's a different woman, this one with glossy auburn hair. How many different women does he buy? He smiles at me, knowing and cruel. Shame curdles my stomach.

"Evening," Gabriel says, guiding me past him up the stairs.

The show has already started. They shouldn't even let us into the theater now. It's against the rules. But of course this is Gabriel Miller. He owns a box. An usher opens the door and gives a polite smile, as if we aren't disheveled and panting, smelling of sex as we stumble into the space.

I take my seat as quickly as possible, but there's no avoiding the stares and whispers. They interrupt the lovely ballroom dance that's happening onstage. I stare at the whirling people, the oversize decorum as if I have no idea that everyone's talking about us.

Finally I chance a glance at Gabriel. He's leaning back in his seat, slouched like a king surveying his subjects. He looks satisfied but still dangerous. A lion in the jungle. Anyone who looks at him like this would know that he just had sex. Maybe not literal sex, but close enough.

But then they'd know that from just looking at me. A little bird in a gilded cage.

Why keep one except to hear her sing?

CHAPTER TWENTY-SIX

MY HAIR IS still wet.

I've only been in bed a few hours. Of course I showered as soon as we got home from the theater, the water scalding, scrubbing the place on my thighs where his come had been. There's no trace of him, but I can still feel the warm spurts, the throb of intense pleasure that he triggered with his come.

Maybe I wouldn't feel so dirty if he'd just taken my virginity the first night. Regular sex, right away. Even coming on me, as sharp and intimate as it is, I could have withstood.

It's the orgasms he forces from my body that feel like a violation.

That's how I find myself getting out of bed at two a.m., twisting the knob all the way to HOT. I stand under the spray for seconds, minute, hours. There's no need for soap, not the physical kind. I just need to forget his fingers around my clit, his breath at the back of my neck.

The hot water heater in this massive house lasts a long time, but it eventually gives up on me. Or maybe it just doesn't want to watch it go down the drain. *This isn't going to help,* the cold water says, stinging my skin. I stand there for as long as I can take, until my teeth are chattering and every part of my skin has pebbled.

Eventually I step out of the shower onto the warm tile. God, even the bathroom tile has warmers. Everything in this place is perfectly modulated for the comfort of the master. For the comfort of Gabriel Miller.

I turn off the shower and dry myself off. A strange sound comes from the room. My hair prickles not from cold but from warning. Animal instinct, the opposite of Gabriel's hands on my sides.

Wrapping the towel tight around me, I peek out the bathroom door.

Nothing.

Maybe I imagined it, just like I imagined the feel of Gabriel's come on my thighs when it had already been washed off, just like I can still hear the whispers and feel the stares of the entire theater.

Then I hear it again, a knocking sound. Not from the door. From the other side of the room.

The window. Pale face. Dark eyes. *Someone looking inside my window.*

I let out a shriek before recognition can slow my heartbeat. God.

Then I'm across the room, shoving open the window, whispering desperately, "Justin! What are you doing here?"

"I'm getting you out of here," he says, his voice grim. He looks different than the last time I saw him. He was never fat, but he'd had the rounded cheeks of a boy who had never had to work very hard. Even sailing hadn't made him lean.

Now he looks more gaunt, his eyes shadowed.

"Through the window? This is crazy."

His eyes flash. "What's crazy is putting yourself up for auction."

His gaze flickers down my body, and I become painfully aware of how little the white towel covers. It hadn't mattered when I thought I was alone in my room. Now he can see the tops of my breasts and most of my legs.

"Please," I say, though I don't know why I'm pleading. For him to leave? For him to understand? He'll never understand. "I didn't have a choice."

He looks away for a moment, and I take in

the fact that he's on a ladder. A ladder. Where did he get it? Some kind of toolshed? Or maybe he brought it with him. This is some insane rescue attempt, except I don't need rescuing.

No, that's a lie. I need rescuing, but I need the money in that escrow account even more.

His nostrils flare. "God, Avery. Why didn't you call me?"

"You broke up with me!"

"Still," he says, seething. "Gabriel Miller! The man ruined your father."

A flush steals over my cheeks, my chest. "I know. I didn't have a choice in who won the auction."

"I can't believe you let him touch you. He turned over fake evidence to the state's attorney. And then he had him attacked! He's the reason your father even needs a nurse."

My heart clenches. "No. He didn't send those men."

"Did you ask him?"

I did, but I'm not sure I believe him. And I'm afraid to push. Afraid to find out that he might have sent those men. Because he won the auction either way. We need the money either way. It's sick and twisted, like the chili juice on my fingers. But sometimes we do sick and twisted things for the people we love.

"It doesn't matter," I say. "The auction is over. He won."

"You're leaving," he says flatly.

"And give up a million dollars? Daddy needs that money." And I needed the house more than ever. The only trace I had left of my mother. She would have known what to do, what to say, but I didn't have her. All I had was the place that she'd lived. The place that she'd loved.

"He doesn't need it from Gabriel Miller. The man's a fucking criminal."

"I know that." My stomach turns over. "But Daddy wasn't innocent either. That came out in the trial."

Justin snorts. "The trial. It was a fucking sham. The whole prosecutor's office is in Miller's pocket."

That's not possible, is it? Daddy maintained his innocence until the end. Until the attack, when he'd almost lost his ability to speak at all. There'd been so much evidence, though.

And Gabriel Miller has more money than God. He can make anything happen.

Except that honesty is the most important thing to him. He keeps his father's last bottle of moonshine to remind him of how much he believes in the truth. He wouldn't have given false documents. Wouldn't have lied to me.

Unless everything was a lie, even his supposed belief in honesty.

I take a step back. "You need to leave."

"Are you listening to me?" he asks, his eyes wild. "The man's a fucking monster."

I had that thought in the theater, but somehow it's different when Justin says it. More offensive. Less true. "You don't know him."

"Oh fuck." Justin laughs. "You aren't falling for him, are you?"

The air seems thin, because I'm terrified that he's right. It's horrible. Impossible. "Of course not. But a deal's a deal. And they take their promises seriously in this criminal business. That's what got Daddy into this mess."

"What do you think they're going to prosecute you for, your virginity? It's fucking gone. Done. Even Gabriel Miller isn't going to bring his whore to court."

I flinch. This was the man I had been going to marry. *Whore.*

"Leave, Justin." I pull the towel tighter around me. "Now."

He seems to realize what he said. "Avery—"

"No. I know you mean well, but this isn't going to work. I need the money from the auction. Daddy needs it. And if Gabriel finds you here, he's going to be pissed."

"Pissed," comes a low voice from behind me. "That's an understatement."

I whirl and face an enraged Gabriel Miller, his face twisted into a snarl. My hands go up in automatic defense. I don't think he's going to hurt me, but he might hurt Justin. However much he betrayed me by breaking off our engagement, he doesn't deserve to be injured.

"Please."

Gabriel looks incredulous. "You're begging for his life?"

Panic beats in my chest. Would Gabriel kill him? "He hasn't done anything."

"He came onto my property. He tried to take what's mine."

Me. He means me. I feel lightheaded. "I'm still here. Please."

He grips my wrist, firm and implacable. He moves me out of the way, and I spin from out of his hold. The towel comes lose, and I use both hands to cover myself.

Two strides. That's all it takes before Gabriel has Justin by the collar, face turning red, his stance on the ladder precarious at best. I run to them, modesty forgotten, pulling Gabriel's arm.

"Let him go!"

Gabriel makes a growling sound. "I'd bury him in the woods. No, I'd leave him out. Let the wolves take care of him. No one would ever find his body."

Justin's eyes are wide and full of fear. "Stop," he wheezes. "Know. The. Truth."

"The truth?" Gabriel asks, his voice deadly soft.

God, doesn't Justin realize how close he is to death? Threatening Gabriel Miller with the truth will only make him angrier. No matter what happened with my father, I know that Gabriel cares about honesty.

And Justin's figuring it out too as the life squeezes out of him. His eyes are glazed over. Gabriel doesn't even have to suffocate him. He only has to let go. Disoriented, dizzy, Justin would fall to his death.

"I'll be good," I promise, my voice low and serious. I'm grasping at Gabriel's white shirt—he hasn't changed, I realize, since the theater. He's still wearing his tuxedo shirt. It doesn't matter how hard I pull, I'll never move him. He's made of stone.

What can I do?

What can I give him?

The string. My very sanity. "I'll play with you. I'll play chess."

Justin makes horrible wheezing sounds, his limbs flailing. For a horrible moment I think he's going to fall, but Gabriel's hold on the front of his shirt keeps him on the ladder.

Gabriel must have loosened his grip, because Justin's eyes come into focus, though his face is still red and puffy. "You bastard," he gasps.

God, he has no survival instinct. "Get out of here," I whisper.

He glances from me to Gabriel and comes to the right conclusion. On unsteady legs he makes it down the ladder. I watch as he runs across the lawn, through the woods where he must have entered. For a moment I worry about wolves, until I realize that I have my own wild animal to think about.

Gabriel turns to me. "Did you call him?"

"What? No! Check the records if you don't believe me."

"Oh, I have," he says grimly. "Mr. Stewart. And Harper St. Claire, your friend from school. You could have sent a message through her."

I'm shaking with anger, realizing that he's been looking at my phone logs. For all I know there's a camera in the room, too. Nothing is sacred to him.

What about the truth? Is that sacred to him? Would he have manufactured evidence for the state's attorney to indict my father? Would he have used bribes to ensure my father's conviction?

My father might be innocent after all.

Gabriel slams the window down and locks it. "We play tomorrow."

CHAPTER TWENTY-SEVEN

I WAKE UP to a note that says only one thing: *3 p.m.*

Which means I have the rest of the day to think about my strategy for the game. I'd rather read a book or watch a movie. I'd rather watch the grass grow, but like with the professor at the museum, I'm too starved for stimulation. My brain has decided to win regardless of what I want.

Well, I wouldn't say that I want to lose. That's not really what this is about, though. This is about giving him a piece of me, opening myself up beyond my body. There are a hundred myths about the way chess play exposes the true identity of a person—a long-lost son reunited with his father by an unusual chess combination alone. Messages written in black and white wood, in an infinite number of moves.

I'll play with Gabriel. I'll play to win, but I won't give up every secret I have.

When I arrive in the library, he already sits in one of the armchairs. The board has been set, with black facing him. He stands when I enter the room, an old-school politeness fitting for a game over a thousand years old.

"Good afternoon," he says.

I eye him warily as I circle the opposite chair, wondering if he's still pissed about Justin. Probably, but he doesn't appear angry today. He has the same bland and solicitous expression that hides everything he's thinking. The perfect poker face.

I wring my hands together. "About Justin."

His face doesn't move a centimeter, but I feel his rage bubble near the surface. "What about him?"

"I need your promise that you won't do anything to him."

He uses that dangerously soft voice he gets when he's lethal. "What would I do to someone like him?"

I force myself to gather my courage, because I couldn't live with myself if Justin ended up hurt. If he ended up like my father. The men in my life were in ruins enough. "Send men to attack him."

He's silent a moment, and all I hear is the faint crackle of the fire. "Is that what you think I did to your father?"

My courage falters, but I force my shoulders back. "Did you?"

"I don't send people to do my dirty work. If I want to beat someone to a pulp, I'll do it myself."

Which doesn't tell me whether he hurt my father. Except my father said they were strangers to him. That there were multiple men, wearing masks. Was that the truth? Or had it been Gabriel Miller?

He looks grave. "And I have no desire to hit an old man."

The relief that fills me is deeper than knowing I'm not in the same room as my father's attacker. It has to do with Gabriel himself. My feelings for him. "You gave the state's attorney evidence about my father."

"It was the most public way to ruin him."

It ruined him. It weakened him enough that somebody else felt comfortable sending men after my father in a dark alley. Maybe it doesn't matter that Gabriel didn't throw the punch himself. He kicked off the chain of events that led to my father in bed, hooked up to a million different machines.

"And to buy his daughter," I say, voice shaking only a little. "In a public auction. Your idea, I remember."

"One of my best ideas."

I don't flinch on the outside. Inside I'm sick with caring about a man who manipulates me like a chess piece. My father? Gabriel? They have that in common, their heavy hands moving me around the board.

The pieces line up, so ordered and polite. The battlefield before there's bloodshed. "I'm white."

"You made the first move," he says because I went to the Den that night.

He's right about that. If I'd never done that, I wouldn't have met Gabriel, wouldn't have been put up for auction, wouldn't be at his estate. Would I change it, if I could? I would have lost the house, the only link to my mother. I would have had to accept Uncle Landon's proposal, trapping myself in a marriage both with a man I think of as family and with a cheater—a man who'd have kept a virgin for a month while engaged to me.

I take a seat and study the board. The pieces are shiny, well polished, not dusty. Obviously hand-carved, expensive, but not especially ornate for a man as rich as Gabriel. He has the home court advantage, but I can infer more from it.

"When did you get this set?"

He smiles briefly. "The day before you arrived. I had it commissioned after the night you visited the Den. Well, a few days later. Once Damon had gotten ahold of your chess teacher's letter."

My eyes widened. "There's no way they could have made it that fast."

"I paid a premium," he says. "I'm not sure the artist slept much."

I look down at the set through new eyes. No one had ever played on this before. The symbolism touches me more than I want it to. A virgin set. Like me. "Why?"

"Call me extravagant."

He is extravagant, but he's also methodical, intelligent. Strategic. Everything he does has a purpose. He must have planned to bid on me from the moment he suggested the auction. Public shame. The ultimate triumph over my father. I should hate him for that, but I can't, any more than I can hate my father for losing.

I move my pawn to e4, a straightforward opening. It doesn't give him any clues about me, but I need to learn something about him if I'm going to win.

He thinks for only a second before moving a pawn to c5. The Sicilian Defense. It doesn't tell me much except that he's not a beginner. If he had done the King's Gambit, I might have been able to lead him along, make him believe he had a chance before ending it. He knows enough to challenge me.

"An interesting game for a mythology major," he murmurs, watching me. "A little aggressive. Mathematical."

If he's trying to distract me it won't work. I move my knight to f3, allowing him to play out his moves before I surprise him. "Actually chess is deeply rooted in mythology. From its many creation stories to the wars that were won and lost with it. Philosophers, kings, poets. People from every walk of life have used chess to explain things."

He smiles and plays again. "You don't believe it was invented by Moses, then?"

Moses is one of many said to have invented the game. The Greek warrior Palamedes created it to demonstrate battle positions. An Indian philosopher designed it to tell the queen that her only son had been assassinated. I'm interested in the truth, but the stories tell us so much about the people throughout history as well.

I move again. "It's not only the myths sur-rounding chess. Chess itself is a myth, you know? A game of hierarchy, of war. It's a story that people have been using to explain complex concepts for eons. Mathematics, yes. Geometry. Business. Philosophy. Even love."

"Love," he says, making a Knight's Gambit. "In a game of war."

I can't tell whether his words are refuting the possibility or marveling at them. Either way I'm not sure I can discuss love with a man who has purchased me like cattle. Or maybe like the brutality of chess, his ownership of me is the perfect myth in which to explore it.

I take his knight. "And if you think archeologists aren't aggressive, you've never seen them fight over a new find."

Our next few moves are done in silence as we fight for control over the board, reaching into the center, establishing our strongholds from which the final battle will be fought.

CHAPTER TWENTY-EIGHT

B Y THE MIDDLE of the game my king is secure in the corner, fortified by the queen, my castles, my knights and strategically placed pawns. It's a strong position that fulfills the most important rule: protection of the king.

In contrast Gabriel has his pieces bleeding into my space—his bishops, his knights. God, even his queen sits on g5, completely in my territory. Seemingly vulnerable, but I can't touch her.

His king is protected by only a single castle and a pawn.

I would be terrified with that little protection, but Gabriel looks confident and assured as usual. Clearly the strategy is deliberate. And as undefended as his king is, I can't touch him.

"Shall we make this game more interesting?" he asks.

Stakes, he means. Betting. "What could I have that you want?"

"You know, little virgin."

My face flames with embarrassment. "You already bought me, remember?"

"I'm talking about a favorable exchange."

I glance at the board suspiciously. Have I left myself in danger? "My queen for your rook?"

He smiles. "No, my queen for your rook."

That would put him in a worse position. "Why would you do that?"

"Your house. It matters to you."

"It's my house. My family's house."

"It's more than that. Tell me why."

"I grew up there. My father is comfortable there, and this might be his last few months." Even that's not the whole truth, and Gabriel knows it.

"He can be comfortable somewhere else."

I stare at the board, trying to think how I can take his queen without answering. I can't. My fists clench helplessly. This is what I didn't want, to be sucked into a battle of wills with Gabriel Miller. To expose the soft flesh where he can hurt me the worst. But then that's the entire point of the chess game.

It's the entire point of a virginity auction, too.

"My mother killed herself."

He sucks in a breath. "I'm sorry."

"My dad told everyone it was an accident.

Stormy night. Faulty brakes. No one questioned it. But I overheard the police chief talking to him that night. There was no sign of anything wrong with her brakes. And the tracks on the road— their forensics determined it was deliberate."

Your mind. Your soul. That's your leverage.

And I'm giving it up in exchange for the truth.

"Avery."

"They kept it quiet because her family, my grandparents, they're Catholic. They wanted her buried in the family crypt. They couldn't have done that if—" If people knew she had killed herself.

"Avery, I'm so sorry."

I've wondered and wondered why she died. Was she scared? Was she angry? I'm a grown woman now but there's a part of me that will always be that broken little girl, wondering why her mother left her, thinking she wasn't good enough to make her stay.

"He built that house for my mother," I say finally. "She conferred with the architect, who designed it for her. I don't know… I don't know why she wanted things that way. Or what it means, if anything. But it's the only thing I have left from her."

"Her chessboard," Gabriel says quietly, surprising me. He moves his queen into jeopardy.

"Yes." It's from the beginning of her marriage with Daddy, when she was hopeful and in love. That was her opening move. And I already know how it ends. But that murky middle game, the place too wild for theoretical constructs. What happened to her then?

I pick up my castle, holding it tight. The wood ridges press into my skin, a pain I find comforting. Then I push aside his queen, capturing her with his consent.

We play the endgame to the sound of a crackling fire for a few minutes. The queen has given me an edge that I might be able to carry into checkmate. Though with his skill he can drag it out for some time, maybe even turn the tables. Unlikely.

I find myself longing to even the score. The queen wasn't a fair trade.

"A favorable exchange," I say.

His eyebrows rise. "Your queen?"

"For your rook. Why did you want my father's business, if it was failing so bad?"

His surprise fills the room, as loud as the fire, as the click of wood against wood. It's a tangible thing, his shock. His reluctance to answer. But he wants my queen. "I saw you," he says slowly. "At your graduation party."

My eyes widen. "You were there?"

"Your father invited me. It would look less conspicuous if I arrived in a crowd. If I were seen dealing with him directly, people would assume we were working together."

I remember the cake shaped like a graduation hat, my elation after four years of preparatory academy uniforms, my excitement over going to college. So full of hope. I'd had no idea that two years later I'd be on the auction block.

And I remember the man on the stairs. "I saw you."

"And I wanted you," Gabriel says.

My breath catches at the raw truth of him. He's exposing himself. It's worth so much more than my queen. "What did you do?"

"I'm not a monster, despite what you think. I could have had you. Could have forced your hand even then. But I wanted you to come to me."

Oh, but he did force my hand. With patience, with cunning. He moved the chess pieces around, blocking me in from behind until there was only one path open to me.

I move my rook out of safety. "That's why you ruined my father," I whisper.

"I'm patient, when I need to be." He captures my queen, turning this into a race to the end. "When your father's business was struggling, he needed a buyer. It was his choice to cheat me."

"That doesn't explain why he invited you to my graduation party in the first place. What were you working on with him? What didn't he want people to know about?"

Gabriel studies the board. "How much do you know about your father?"

"I went to the trial." Even though it had felt like a punch in the gut, every dark revelation about him, every former colleague that stood on the witness stand to testify against him. So many secrets. "I heard what he did."

"Not everything."

"Then what?"

"Your bishop," he says softly.

I look down at the board, denial in my hands, my arms. Clenched in my chest. I can still win this. I know I can, and I think he knows it too. Except if I give him my bishop, I'll be leaving my king exposed. Checkmate in two moves. I'll lose. How much is this information worth to me?

My heart beats a frantic rhythm as I reach the end.

I move the bishop into jeopardy.

"I've known your father for years. Who he is.

But I hadn't worked with him before. He invited me to your graduation party to see if I'd be willing to work with him, like my father did."

Dread is a cold fist around my heart. "What did your father do with him?"

"He bought things. Sold things." Gabriel uses his knight to take my queen. Only one move left and he'll have my king. "Like most businessmen do."

Except that his father was a liar, which is why Gabriel hated him so much. "Drugs. Guns?"

Golden eyes meet mine. "People."

I suck in a breath, horrified, disbelieving. "No."

He means that his father dealt in human trafficking. That my father had too.

"Move," Gabriel says softly.

My fingers feel numb as I nudge a pawn forward. I ought to just knock over my king. I know what's coming, but I need to hear him say it. I need to know the truth. Maybe I'm just like Gabriel Miller, after all. Myths can tell you about the people who make them, who believe them, but it's the truth that matters.

His rook crosses the board to the first row. *Checkmate.*

The word comes from ancient Persian. Some say it means the King is dead, but the translation is a little less dire—depending on how you look at it. The King is helpless. The King is defeated. When there are no moves left, the only option is surrender.

"I don't deal in people," he says. "I made that promise to myself when my father died. Never. Not ever. And then you were there, desperate and broke. God, you'd actually gotten thinner."

"You could have helped me!"

"That's not how this works."

The auction had been brutal. Being purchased like an object. The brief moments of kindness he gives me. "You bought me, but you haven't fucked me."

"Is it killing you, the wait? Are you imagining the worst-case scenario with that beautiful strategic brain of yours? Would it be better if I came to your room tonight and broke you, little virgin?"

Yes, God help me. I can't manage words, and it comes out as a sob. My father was the monster in the Labyrinth all along. That's who I put my virginity on the auction block for, someone who had bought and sold people. That's what had paid for my tuition, my fancy dresses. I feel sick. Did my mother know about this? Was this why she killed herself?

The last thing I see before I flee from the room is my king, fallen over on the board.

Chapter Twenty-Nine

I PRESS MY forehead against the cool glass, looking out at the dark woods. Justin braved those woods, and maybe actual wolves, to rescue me. It was actually pretty gallant, if not very well-thought-out. Gabriel would have gotten revenge on him in a manner both public and thorough.

And I'd have given up a million dollars. Maybe it would have been worth it for love. But Justin had proven this wasn't love when he broke up with me for what my father did.

So I'm still here, still locked in the tower with my very own dragon.

Gabriel is right when he said my mind can imagine the worst. A hundred strategies, a million possibilities. All the things he might do to me.

Why do I wait for him to come to me?

He gave me white because I made the first move. That's what I should do about sex. It's an advantage—a small one, but I need any advantage I can get. In chess we're well matched. I still lost, sacrificing the game to get information that broke my heart. But when it comes to sex, he's the far superior player. I'm a novice. I'm nothing.

But I will finish this game the way I started it—with courage.

I know exactly which room to find him in. The only door that's locked. Who keeps the bedroom locked in their own house? A person with something to hide.

My footsteps are soundless on the oriental runner in the hallway. My knock echoes, incongruously loud. It sounds aggressive. That's what he said about chess. Aggressive and mathematical. That's how I feel right now, as if I'm making the devil's bargain.

He opens the door, his expression incredulous. "You."

His shirtsleeves are rolled up, his dress pants revealing black socks. That seems like suddenly intimate knowledge, those black socks. I've already seen so much more of his body—felt it, anyway, in the darkness of the spiral staircase— but the simple domesticity of his socked feet seems momentous.

"Can I come in?"

He laughs, leaving the door open as he strides back into the room. That's when I realize that he's drunk. There's a bottle on the table by his fire-place. I recognize the fading ink, the clear liquid. Moonshine.

I follow him inside and shut the door behind us.

He lifts a half-empty glass in mock salute. "Want some?"

"Maybe it's best if one of us stays sober."

His throat moves as he takes a large swallow. "I'm not that drunk. Not too drunk to get it up, if that's what you came here for."

I blink. It takes me one, two, three seconds to figure out what he means by *it* and *up*. It's embarrassing that I didn't know there is a too drunk for sex. "Good."

A rough laugh. "Oh, little virgin. You're so delicious. Do you know that?"

My cheeks heat, and I turn away. "Not for much longer."

There's a soft *clink* that must be him setting down his glass. A stir of air as he comes close. The faintest brush of the back of his fingers against my cheek. "You'll always be delicious."

I meet his gaze. "But not a virgin."

"No," he says, considering. "I don't think you'll be one for very long. Did you come to make a trade? A favorable exchange?"

"I don't have anything left to bargain with." He's taken my body in every way but this. And he's taken what I swore never to give him: my mind, my soul. The ball of string that would have shown me the way out. There's nothing left.

He pulls something from his pocket, examining it. The pale wood gleams in the firelight. A pawn. He must have brought it from downstairs. I remember the shape of it, the smooth surface beneath my fingertips.

"So small," he says, voice thick. "Why can't I let you go?"

He must be drunker than he thinks if he's talking to a piece of carved wood. Unless he means me. "I'm right here."

His golden gaze focuses on me. "Yes, little virgin. Will you undress for me? Will you open your legs? Let me fuck you until you bleed like a goddamn martyr?"

A tremble begins from deep in my chest, spreading outward to my limbs. "I know you can make it good for me."

"You don't want *good*," he says as if the word itself is filthy. "You want to be fucked. That's why you came here. Say it."

My voice is a whisper. "I came here to be fucked."

He points to the bed. "Sit."

I sit on the edge of the bed, realizing only when my feet dangle that it's so tall. I feel small and helpless, which was probably the point. On edge. Definitely the point.

That's when I realize what he's doing. I made the first move. He could have matched me, but that would have been too easy. Instead he moves the game in a different direction, expands the circle of our battle. The Sicilian Defense. It's what he did with the auction, and it's what he's doing now.

He comes to stand in front of me, his large hand toying with the ruffles of my nightgown. "What is this?"

I bite my lip, embarrassed. "My other pajamas have...well, pictures. Unicorns. Rainbows." I'm not really that childlike, but they were funny. Playful. This nightgown is a pale cream with a small pink bow at the neck. Too modest to seduce anyone, but better than monkeys in sunglasses.

He studies the ruffles as if he's never seen them before. They may as well be a new move in chess theory for how much they take his concentration—the little flurry of fabric, the inch of thigh underneath. "You hurt me, you know."

"What?"

"Whenever I think about you, I hurt." He puts a hand to his chest. "Here."

For a second I think he might be mocking me, like the men in the auction did. It's a cold splash of water on arousal that shouldn't be there. But he looks deadly serious.

And he always tells the truth.

"That's the moonshine talking," I say, pressing my knees together.

He draws a line down my legs, where they touch. "This is the sexiest thing I've ever seen."

Not my breasts or my ass. It's the seam of my legs, the line that keeps him out.

He wants a chess game. That's why he bought me. That's why he waited to take my virginity. I don't know whether the other men wanted my body or my soul, but this man—he wants the challenge.

I look away because it's scarier to play the game. *Don't fight him, oppose him. Make him desperate for more.* That's what Candy told me. I remember the knowing look in her eyes, the challenge. She knew how much harder this would be, to participate instead of fighting. To try to win knowing I'll most likely lose.

I want to be the martyr, like he said. I need that, because it's the only way I can hate him.

Make me bleed. Make me cry. I'd despise him in pure righteous fury.

It's the kindness I can't trust.

His thumb turns my chin to face him. "Little virgin."

"Gabriel."

"Spread your legs."

My heart pounds. "Make me."

There's that pawn again. He rubs his finger over it in a way that shouldn't be sensual but is. Again and again, until the smooth curved head seems like a place on my body. Until every stroke of his thumb makes me clench. "Don't you want this?" he murmurs.

It would be easy for him to push his hand between my legs, to spread them for me. I couldn't stop him. I wouldn't try. He wants me to give in, though. He wants to line up his pieces, prepared to strike. And then he wants me to move my queen into jeopardy, because he asks.

"No."

He laughs softly, considering the rounded head of the pawn. "Such a small thing. But powerful. Don't you think?"

His tongue swipes his thumb, which he uses on the pawn again. It glistens with his saliva. Then he does something obscene, something shocking—he puts the curved pawn against his lips. A kiss. The hint of a lick. "Open."

My legs are trembling with the force of staying together. My inner thigh muscles are clenching and unclenching, spasming as I watch him suck the little head of the piece.

My breath catches. "I can't—"

Every cell in my body is screaming for me to open my thighs, but it's not just his thumb that will touch me. Not just his lips or his tongue. He'll fuck me tonight. The promise is burning bright in his gaze.

"You have to, little virgin. It's the only way you'll feel better. Just give in."

Move into jeopardy. Be captured. So simple and yet so hard to do. *Surrender.*

My fists clench in the sheets behind me. Slowly, centimeter by centimeter, I open my legs to him. Two of his fingers lift the frill at the bottom of my nightgown, studying me with humiliating frankness.

"Such a beautiful pussy. Is it beautiful because no one has fucked it yet? Or is it fuckable because it's so beautiful?"

I have to laugh. "Now that's definitely the moonshine talking."

His grin is dark and playful. Seductive. "The

moonshine is a nice excuse to say what I'm thinking. God, little virgin. If you knew what I thought about, watching you in that gold dress, seeing you in those godforsaken yoga pants. Prancing around the house like you feel safe. I want to bring you down like a fucking gazelle in the Serengeti."

My eyes feel wide, my breath faster. My legs spread a little farther apart.

"Keep your hands in the sheets," he says softly.

"Okay," I gasp.

"Yes, sir."

There's a fight inside me. *The string, hold onto the string!* But I want so badly to surrender. I need to. My eyes close on a sigh. "Yes, sir."

Blunt fingers push my thigh to the side even farther. I'm so exposed like this. Vulnerable. Then he touches my clit, like I wanted him to. My body shudders against the caress.

Except it feels different. Harder. Cooler.

I look down to see him holding the pawn, pressing it against me. "Oh God," I whisper.

"I love those ridiculous ruffles, but I need you to take that off now. Unless you want me to come all fucking over it."

It's hard to move, hard to breathe when he's

doing that with the chess piece against my clit. Clumsy arms manage to work their way out of the nightgown. I push it over my flushed face, not even minding the stark nakedness that follows, his hungry gaze on my breasts. It all feeds the intensity building between my legs, centered on that horrible little chess piece. The one he caressed. *The one he licked.*

My body responds to the hardness of the wood, the curve of the head, but I want something else. Heat. Velvet. His body, muscled and hair roughened. The pawn feels impersonal, demeaning, and God, even sexier because of it. There's a darker seduction in knowing he's once removed from me. The pawn is a tool, and so am I. My head drops back, eyes staring at nothing, hips rocking into the piece.

"That's right," he murmurs. "Come all over the pawn. Spill your sweet juice on it. I want to lick you up like that. I want you nice and wet for what happens next."

What happens next, what happens next. The words bounce around in my head, meaningless. Until the sound of a zipper tears through the room. Then my gaze snaps to his pants, where he's taken out his cock. He's stroking it. And it's big. Massive. A million times bigger than the pawn. How will it go inside me? Why wasn't I satisfied with the small wooden head on my clit? He's got a club in his fist.

"Wait," I say, the word slurred with impending climax. "Wait, please."

"Naughty, little virgin. There's no waiting." He makes the circles faster, tighter, pressing the pawn right where I need it. Then I'm crying out, sobbing, begging him to stop, give me, no, more, *please.*

The spasms continue long after he pulls the chess piece away. He doesn't just lick me up. He puts the whole head of the pawn into his mouth, sucking me off the wood before tossing the pawn aside.

Then there's something thick and blunt at my entrance.

"How?" I ask, almost frantic with the question. How will he fit? How did I come to this? How will I go on after this, knowing that I sold my soul to the devil?

He doesn't give me an answer but pushes inside with one hard thrust.

The cry that escapes me is primal—grief at losing something. Pain at the violation. "Gabriel."

"A little more," he says, teeth gritted.

That's when I realize he isn't all the way inside. "Oh God. I can't take more."

"You knew it would hurt," he murmurs, jaw tight, eyes shut as if he's hanging on to control by a thread.

I shouldn't care about him, shouldn't love what he does to me. That's how he's broken me. So much worse than the ripping agony in my body. So much harder than knowing we'll end when the clock stops ticking. "Do it," I whisper.

He takes the invitation with a curt nod. There's a slight tensing of his muscles. I feel it between my legs. That's the only warning before he pushes forward, plunging deep inside me. I can feel him at my very center, filling me, *hurting me*. "How do people do this?"

His laugh is pained. "Only you could make me smile at a time like this."

I wince. "Is it over?"

He reaches down and uses his thumb like he promised, rubbing it over my clit like the smooth head of the pawn. Around and around in endless, blissful circles. By degrees I can relax. It still feels too full. There's a memory of the burn as he entered me. But my muscles ripple around in something almost like pleasure.

Then he pulls back and pushes in, hitting a spot inside me that makes my back arch, my head bend back, my teeth click together in audible shock.

"That's right, little virgin," he says, one syllable between every thrust.

I'm turning into some other creature, more and more every time he finds that place inside me. My whole body feels liquid, turned inside out. Something is building, like when he touches my clit but different too. "I'm not...a virgin...anymore."

He's inside me, so deep inside me.

One thrust and he's all the way to the hilt. I can feel the coarse hairs of him pressing against my sensitive bare skin. He grinds there, and my eyes roll back.

"Did you really think this would end?" he mutters roughly. "Did you think I would fuck you and you'd stop being my little virgin?"

I don't answer. I can't. He's rocking against my clit with his whole body, and it's pushing me over some edge. I dig my heels into his back, desperate to hold on to the ledge.

"No, I bought your virginity. I took it. It's mine, little virgin. Just like you, you're mine."

My mouth opens on an uneven breath. He pushes his hips against mine, a crude demand my body understands better than I do. The orgasm hits me, and I'm freefalling, dizzy with it, upside down, the wind against my face. I can see the high ledge that I'd stood on as I reach the ground and crash.

Gabriel grabs the back of my neck with one hand, my hip with the other. Leverage, I realize. My body and soul. One. Two. Three deep thrusts and then he's coming, groaning like he's in pain, muttering my name in rapid succession—*Avery, Avery. Fuck, Avery.*

He collapses on me, rolling to the side, pulling me with him.

And then one final "Fuck," his voice broken.

"I didn't know," I whisper, and it feels like a grave injustice that it took until the ripe age of twenty to learn how this could feel. At the same time it's the perfect discovery. "I didn't know you could be so deep inside."

There's a strange emptiness when he pulls out of me, a dampness against my thigh. Then I'm draped over him, catching my breath against his broad chest, reeling from what just happened.

CHAPTER THIRTY

I'M STILL BREATHING hard when he stands up.

He touches something on the sheet. Blood, bright and smeared across white sheets. It looks barbaric. That came from my body. From his rough claiming.

His hand curls into a fist.

"Gabriel?"

Without a word he goes into the bathroom. I'm half expecting him to draw a bath like he did for me before. Or maybe return with a damp towel. I can feel him between my legs.

It's sore there. And bloody, apparently.

The sweat on my body cools, and I shiver in the bed. Alone.

I feel a little disoriented, as if I drank a whole bottle of that moonshine. What just happened? That was sex. I just had sex with Gabriel Miller. I lost my virginity to him.

My legs are unsteady as I stand, using the side table to hold myself up until my knees lock. Then

I make my way over to the bathroom, where the door is slitted open. Gabriel is standing there naked, unselfconscious, his arms braced on the edge of the counter, his strange gold gaze trained on the mirror. He's looking at himself. What does he see?

"Gabriel?"

He doesn't move. "What do you want?"

The sharpness of his voice cuts me. "Are you coming back to bed?"

I liked the way he held me last time, curled around me protectively while I drifted off to sleep. I need him to do that again, especially with the strange, remote expression on his face.

"It's my bed," he says, voice brusque. "I belong there. Not you."

I suck in a breath. "Why are you being like this?"

"Like what?"

"Like an ass!"

"I'm sorry if you were expecting something different, Ms. James. I bought you. I used you. Now I'm done."

Stung, I take a step back. "So I'm supposed to go to my room and sit there until you want to *use* me again, is that it?"

He swings around to face me, taking a step

closer. "No, I don't want to use you anymore. Now that I've had you, I'm done. You can go."

My mouth drops. "But…a month…"

His gaze flickers over my body, both admiring and cruel. "You're beautiful, but there are lots of beautiful women in the city. The only thing that made you special was your virginity, and now that's gone."

Hurt feels like a concrete block in my chest, weighing me down, making it impossible to breathe. "You're just saying that."

"Why would I just say that?" he asks, mocking. "Do you really think that highly of yourself? One taste and I would have to keep fucking you for eternity? That's a pretty magical cunt you must have."

Rage feels so much better than the aching pain. "Fine. Pretend like there wasn't a connection between us. Pretend like you didn't enjoy the chess and the…the sex!"

Two steps and he's right in front of me. Then his hand fists in my hair. He bends my head back so I'm looking up at him. "Let's get this straight, Ms. James. I enjoyed the chess. I enjoyed the sex even more. But you were only a means to an end. A pawn."

I blink, but there's no fighting these tears.

They fill my eyes and fall in shameful drops down my cheeks. He lets go of my hair with a rough sound.

"We got too close," I say, my voice uneven. "You're scared, because—"

"Make excuses for me. Because Daddy kept a whorehouse, I never learned how to love, is that it? Tell me, little virgin. Did you imagine you could fix me? Did you think if you beat me at chess, I'd learn my lesson? But I won the game, didn't I? You lost."

Through the tears I see the beige pawn lying on the carpet. Discarded. Its usefulness over. That's what I am here—my father's daughter, bought to send a message. Fucked to drive that message home. He's nothing if not thorough. And now my usefulness? It's over.

I stare at his back as he walks into the bedroom, dismissing me.

He picks up the half-empty bottle of moonshine from the table.

How could I have cared about him? But it doesn't matter. I still care about him, even now that I know he's every bit the monster I feared. The heart is the cruelest enemy of all.

With my heart in my throat, I move to leave. I'm standing with my hand on the knob, trying to make sense of it. I spent so long thinking about defeating the Minotaur that I didn't consider he might just let me go.

I didn't consider that I would have liked to stay.

Part of me wants to go to him, to demand that he explain why he's kicking me out, to make him see we have something deeper. Except I barely know that myself. It's a shock to realize I've come to care for him, this man of precious metal and revenge, of carved wood and heartache.

I'm supposed to hate him.

From across the room comes a terrible crash, making me jump. I turn to see the thick moonshine bottle in shards against the iron grate in the fireplace, a ship against jagged rocks, embattled by the storm.

Gabriel destroyed it, that last memento from his father.

How had I forgotten his violence? Why had I been so sure he wouldn't use it against me? Fear runs through my veins, cold and thin. I may not hate Gabriel Miller, but I'm still afraid of him. Then I'm running through the halls, trying to remember my way back, trying to find the way out.

CHAPTER THIRTY-ONE

I'D LIKE TO slink away in silent disgrace, but I don't have a car. I also don't have the address to call a cab. I consider using my phone's location to request an Uber, but I'm pretty sure there's a fence around the property. I don't need another confrontation like the one with Justin.

So in a humiliating walk of shame, I head downstairs.

The kitchen is empty, but I find Mrs. Burchett in a room off to the side, reading a book. She stands as soon as she sees me. "Oh, hello, dear. Are you hungry? I can heat up…" Then her shrewd eyes take in my expression. She makes a *tsk* sound. "What do you need, dear?"

"I think…a cab." I flush, ashamed because surely my hair and rumpled clothes give away what I've just done. I probably even smell like sex. "He said I should go."

She shakes her head as if admonishing Gabriel. "I'll call a car around."

"No, just a cab—"

Her lips purse together. "He'll want to make sure you're safe."

"I wouldn't count on that," I mutter.

She types something into her phone, clearly as proficient with an iPhone as she is with a rolling pin. "I know he can be a bear, but he does care about you."

I flinch. He's just made it abundantly clear that he doesn't, but I have no desire to spell it out for Mrs. Burchett. *That's a pretty magical cunt you must have.* "It doesn't matter."

"Oh, but it does," she insists. "He made sure your father was taken care of. It damn near killed him to wait until that night to send someone to help you."

"He had to. The auction—"

"Gabriel Miller doesn't have to do anything. He set the terms because he knew you needed help. That's why he sent someone to watch over you, once he heard there was someone watching you." She casts a worried glance into the dark night. "Imagine he'll do the same now that you're going back."

"You're wrong. That guard was from Damon, protecting his investment."

She clearly doesn't believe me. "Well, you be

careful regardless. The world is full of dangerous people, Ms. James."

Headlights flash from the drive.

That's the story of how I end up in a limo two hours after I lost my virginity.

The driver doesn't ask any questions, for which I'm grateful. I cross my arms in front of me, holding tight as if I can keep myself from breaking into a thousand different pieces.

I'm not sure what I thought I'd be returning to when I left for the auction. Some chance at a normal life? College? Marriage? It all feels so far removed. Impossible words. I've lost the ball of string somewhere along the way. I might be going home, but I'm still in the maze.

All I have with me is my purse. Mrs. Burchett assured me that my clothes and things would be delivered tomorrow. *He'll want to make sure you have everything right away.* Or maybe he'd just throw it all into the fire like his father's moonshine.

I pull out my phone, trying to pretend I'm not looking for his name. I want him to call me, to tell me he's sorry. But he doesn't. There are lots of missed calls. None from him.

Almost unthinking I press the last name. Harper.

"Where have you been?" she demands.

"I—" My voice breaks, because I don't know how to explain. I don't even understand it myself. Almost every myth references love, betrayal. Heartbreak. Universal truths that I've read a thousand times but still can't comprehend. No story can explain this pain that feels too big for my body.

"Justin is missing."

Awareness rises like the tide, slow but ineffable. "What do you mean?"

"I mean he never went back to Yale. I know a couple guys over there. One who's on the sailing team with him. He went AWOL."

"He came to see me, but…"

Gabriel swore he wouldn't hurt him. Or did he? I can't be sure I got the promise from him. Where would Justin have gone if not back to school? He might have stayed at his parents' house in Tanglewood, but he would have at least texted his teammates. Even with winter creeping up, they continued to sail.

I drop the phone onto the seat. It slides onto the floor as the limo stops.

When the car stops at the gate, I already have the door open.

Lights are on in the house when my father's

evening routine should be finished. No one should be here. A man in a suit emerges from the front door. I run toward the house, my heart pounding with a new fear.

"Ms. James?" he asks.

"That's me. What's going on?" I try to push past him, but he's blocking my path. "Where's my father?"

"I'm Mr. Stewart. We spoke on the phone."

That catches my attention. Pushing past the panic, I focus on him—on the solemn expression in his eyes. He looks as kind as he sounded on the phone. And worried.

"Oh God. No."

"Your father suffered a coronary incident this evening. He's been taken to Tanglewood Hospital. I don't have the details yet, but our emergency staff is interfacing with the doctors there to make sure he has the best care."

He's been standing in front of the door, and as I turn my head, I see something yellow affixed to the thick wood. It pulls me closer, almost as if I'm hypnotized. Mr. Stewart is still talking, something about complications and interventions, but he's just background noise.

In bold letters the yellow paper says NOTICE OF CRIMINAL FORFEITURE.

"How is that possible?" I whisper.

The house is owned by my trust, which is owned by me. Uncle Landon said it would be safe. From the very beginning, he told me that. Protected from my father's crimes. The auction would have covered the real estate taxes, the maintenance—except it's too late.

Somehow I'm too late.

The expression of sympathy on Mr. Stewart's face is the worst thing I've ever seen. Worse than the cruel look on Gabriel's face when he said the words *magic cunt*. "We received a call yesterday that Mr. James would be required to vacate the premises."

"Did Daddy know?" My voice cracks. "Did he know we'd lost the house?"

A grim pause. "He knew."

There's only one question. "Who?"

Did Uncle Landon find a way to break through the trust, his revenge for choosing the auction over his proposal? It hurts to think about, but maybe that's not the answer. Maybe it's much more obvious—and much more painful. Did Gabriel Miller figure out a way to circumvent the trust and take ownership of the house?

I look down at the yellow sheet of paper, already crushed in my fists. I smooth it open as if

SKYE WARREN

it's an ancient scroll, the secrets of lost treasure written on parchment. There's legalese about vacating the premises—that's what my mother's legacy has been reduced to, premises.

And then I see it, the holding company with a corporate address.

Miller Industries.

That's Gabriel Miller's company. Which means he now has possession of this house. Did he engineer this entire thing? A ruthless takeover, except this isn't business. It's personal. He must have known what I would find when he sent me away.

And he had hired Mr. Stewart. Gabriel might have known about my father's coronary, too. Had he sent me home as some twisted kindness, knowing my father would need me now?

But I won the game, didn't I? You lost.

No, Gabriel doesn't know how to be kind.

I latch on to the only hope I have. "There has to be something we can do. Fight it. Appeal. This is my *house*. My mother's house."

Mr. Stewart shakes his head. "You'll have to speak to a lawyer."

A lawyer, like the kind who couldn't save my father from disgrace. The kind who made sure he paid every cent he owned in restitution and

286

penalties. They won't help us. "What happens?" I say, desperate now. "You must have seen this before. What happens to the house?"

"It depends," he says slowly. "But in these cases, where the house is taken to settle payments owed, it will be put up for sale. It will be put up for auction."

My heart clenches hard. Put up for auction, like my body. Like everything about my life, for sale to the highest bidder. I already sold my virginity, but it didn't matter. I still lost the house. And my father might die.

Checkmate.

THE END

THANK YOU!

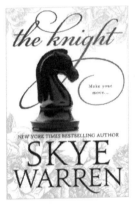

Thank you for reading THE PAWN! I hope you love Gabriel and Avery. Their story continues in THE KNIGHT! Find out what happens when she returns to fight for her family.

The power of pleasure...

Gabriel Miller took everything from me. My family. My innocence. My home. The only thing I have left is the determination to get back what's mine.

He thinks he's beaten me. He thinks he's won. What he doesn't realize is that every pawn has the chance to become a queen.

And the game has only just begun.

SIGN UP FOR SKYE WARREN'S NEWSLETTER: www.skyewarren.com/newsletter

And don't miss the brand new release!

Forbidden fruit never tasted this sweet...

> *"Swoon-worthy, forbidden, and sexy, Liam North is my new obsession."*
>
> – New York Times bestselling author
> Claire Contreras

The world knows Samantha Brooks as the violin prodigy. She guards her secret truth—the desire she harbors for her guardian.

Liam North got custody of her six years ago. She's all grown up now, but he still treats her like a child. No matter how much he wants her.

No matter how bad he aches for one taste.

> *"Overture is a beautiful composition of forbidden love and undeniable desire. Skye has crafted a gripping, sensual, and intense story that left me breathless. Get ready to be hooked!"*
>
> – USA Today bestselling author Nikki
> Sloane

Turn the page for an excerpt from OVERTURE...

EXCERPT FROM OVERTURE

*R*EST, LIAM TOLD me.

He's right about a lot of things. Maybe he's right about this. I climb onto the cool pink sheets, hoping that a nap will suddenly make me content with this quiet little life.

Even though I know it won't.

Besides, I'm too wired to actually sleep. The white lace coverlet is both delicate and comfy. It's actually what I would have picked out for myself, except I didn't pick it out. I've been incapable of picking anything, of choosing anything, of deciding anything as part of some deep-seated fear that I'll be abandoned.

The coverlet, like everything else in my life, simply appeared.

And the person responsible for its appearance? Liam North.

I climb under the blanket and stare at the ceiling. My body feels overly warm, but it still feels good to be tucked into the blankets. The blankets *he* picked out for me.

It's really so wrong to think of him in a sexual way. He's my guardian, literally. Legally. And he has never done anything to make me think he sees *me* in a sexual way.

This is it. This is the answer.

I don't need to go skinny dipping in the lake down the hill. Thinking about Liam North in a sexual way is my fast car. My parachute out of a plane.

My eyes squeeze shut.

That's all it takes to see Liam's stern expression, those fathomless green eyes and the glint of dark blond whiskers that are always there by late afternoon. And then there's the way he touched me. My forehead, sure, but it's more than he's done before. That broad palm on my sensitive skin.

My thighs press together. They want something between them, and I give them a pillow. Even the way I masturbate is small and timid, never making a sound, barely moving at all, but I can't change it now. I can't moan or throw back my head even for the sake of rebellion.

But I can push my hips against the pillow, rocking my whole body as I imagine Liam doing more than touching my forehead. He would trail his hand down my cheek, my neck, my shoulder.

Repressed. I'm so repressed it's hard to imagine more than that.

I make myself do it, make myself trail my hand down between my breasts, where it's warm and velvety soft, where I imagine Liam would know exactly how to touch me.

You're so beautiful, he would say. *Your breasts are perfect.*

Because Imaginary Liam wouldn't care about big breasts. He would like them small and soft with pale nipples. That would be the absolute perfect pair of breasts for him.

And he would probably do something obscene and rude. Like lick them.

My hips press against the pillow, almost pushing it down to the mattress, rocking and rocking. There's not anything sexy or graceful about what I'm doing. It's pure instinct. Pure need.

The beginning of a climax wraps itself around me. Claws sink into my skin. There's almost certain death, and I'm fighting, fighting, fighting for it with the pillow clenched hard.

"Oh fuck."

The words come soft enough someone else might not hear them. They're more exhalation of breath, the consonants a faint break in the sound.

I have excellent hearing. Ridiculous, crazy good hearing that had me tuning instruments before I could ride a bike.

My eyes snap open, and there's Liam, standing there, frozen. Those green eyes locked on mine. His body clenched tight only three feet away from me. He doesn't come closer, but he doesn't leave.

Orgasm breaks me apart, and I cry out in surprise and denial and relief. "*Liam.*"

It goes on and on, the terrible pleasure of it. The wrenching embarrassment of coming while looking into the eyes of the man who raised me for the past six years.

Want to read more? OVERTURE is available on Amazon, iBooks, Barnes & Noble, Kobo, and other book retailers!

More Books by Skye Warren

Trust Fund Duet

Survival of the Richest

The Evolution of Man

North Security series

Overture

Concerto

Sonata

Underground series

Rough

Hard

Fierce

Wild

Dirty

Secret

Sweet

Deep

Stripped series

Tough Love

Love the Way You Lie

Better When It Hurts

Even Better

Pretty When You Cry

Caught for Christmas

Hold You Against Me

To the Ends of the Earth

Standalone Books

Wanderlust

On the Way Home

Beauty and the Beast

Anti Hero

Escort

About the Author

Skye Warren is the New York Times bestselling author of contemporary romance such as the Chicago Underground and Stripped series. Her books have been featured in Jezebel, Buzzfeed, USA Today Happily Ever After, Glamour, and Elle Magazine. She makes her home in Texas with her loving family, two sweet dogs, and one evil cat.

Sign up for Skye's newsletter:
www.skyewarren.com/newsletter

Like Skye Warren on Facebook:
facebook.com/skyewarren

Join Skye Warren's Dark Room reader group:
skyewarren.com/darkroom

Follow Skye Warren on Instagram:
instagram.com/skyewarrenbooks

Visit Skye's website for her current booklist:
www.skyewarren.com/books

COPYRIGHT

This is a work of fiction. Any resemblance to actual persons, living or dead, business establishments, events or locales is entirely coincidental. All rights reserved. Except for use in a review, the reproduction or use of this work in any part is forbidden without the express written permission of the author.

65310239R00179